STUCK LIKE LINT

SHEFALI TRIPATHI MEHTA

olive turtle

NIYOGI BOOKS

Published by
NIYOGI BOOKS
Block D, Building No. 77,
Okhla Industrial Area, Phase-I,
New Delhi-110 020, INDIA
Tel: 91-11-26816301, 26818960
Email: niyogibooks@gmail.com
Website: www.niyogibooksindia.com

Editor: Jayalakshmi Sengupta
Design: Misha Oberoi

ISBN: 978-93-85285-81-3
Publication: 2017

Printed at: Niyogi Offset Pvt. Ltd., New Delhi, India

To Mummy and Papa
for the childhood spent wandering
as much outside as in the head

—why all this beating of wings?
What was this cage, invisible to us,
which she felt herself to be confined in?
Well there are many ways of being held prisoner…
—Anne Carson, *The Glass Essay*

T's new book came in the morning post.

It's midnight, and I'm still unable to come to terms with what has happened.

Am I angry? Yes. So angry, I could smash some dinner plates. That incidentally is what T said I should do when I was having a rough time with an author. 'Go to the kitchen, take out your nice dinner plates and, one by one, drop them on the floor; watch them go to pieces,' she had winked.

That was T as I knew her—holding life before her with both her hands, looking it in the eye, loving and embracing it with her big, giving heart; challenging it too.

I still remember it was a gorgeous March morning, a day after Holi when I got her manuscript from the publisher; I read it at one go and instantly loved the author. She needed an editor alright. She was in too much of a hurry while writing. Over the years, I would ask her if no English teacher ever rapped her knuckles when she wrote unnecessary capitals and exclamation marks.

'You also need to earn your bread and butter, no?' She would tease me. For the longest time, I called her 'Ms Bread and Butter' to which she would say, 'Wait till I become famous and then I'll be your 'Ms Champagne and Caviar.' Her sparkling humour, her robust positivity—that's what I loved most about her.

A Sight To Dream

He stood in his grand form—six feet six and three across—at the open door of our Diwali home, twinkling with fairy lights and diyas, white Lakshmi-feet alpana at the threshold, and bandanwars of marigolds and mango leaves over the doors; table tops loaded with mithai and dry fruit, and two dozen faces, including those of a husband, his parents, his brothers and sisters, two uncles, one neighbour, spouses of some, nephews, and nieces, turned towards him. And he said—what would have sounded fantastic in a dream—'I have come for you'—looking straight at me, sitting at the edge of the diwan in my moss green bandhani saree with gota patti, of which he had said, looking at the WhatsApp pic I'd sent him earlier, that he could feel the sequins as he imagined me crushed in his arms.

The ogre of my nightmares had finally chased me to the precipice of my existence. I could take a free fall till I crashed to the bottom or be ripped apart, body and soul, slowly, smoulderingly, the poison released into my soul like a drug's sustained relief—for life.

I had to choose my escape.

Coffee Break

She called me to the cafe next to my office. I was surprised. In the six months I'd returned from England, I hadn't seen her at a single play like I did before. Two years ago, she was a regular. Shyamli. Not beautiful in the conventional sense, but very attractive. A lot of the waiting crowd at the lobby always gravitated towards her and there was no doubt that she had a long line of admirers. I did not want to be thought of as one, so initially I stayed away.

However, at one such show, as I was coming out of the men's loo, I saw her with my dad. She was listening to him, a theatre critic, in rapt attention. I was obliged to walk up to them. Dad introduced us. I saw how her eyes glinted like liquid diamonds when she smiled. She spoke little but was extremely courteous. That night, I recall, I could not sleep because her face lingered before my eyes. I started reading her blog. The maturity and depth in her critiques made me 'follow' it, anonymously, of course.

I could see her even before I entered the cafe. That's how she is—a showstopper, as some say. She sat fashionably sprawled over the red leather sofa, her long limbs crossed elegantly at the ankles, smiling. I thought she had seen me, but as I entered and walked up to her, I realised there was someone else she was smiling at—a little girl in a lemon yellow smocked frock, blabbering as she stood holding the table for support, tottering on her pudgy legs.

Shyamli took my hand in a warm handshake.

'Long time.'

'Yeah. I'm just back in town.'

'I know.'

A little tentatively, she moved closer and gave me a quick hug. I was surprised. She turned to pick up the gurgling child in her arms and sat down with her on the lap. I sat down too.

'How have you been?'

'Good. See!' she pointed to the child, as if she was pointing to the source of all goodness.

The child trying to free herself from Shyamli's grip began to whimper. Shyamli set her down by the table again, and the little girl, watching me see her stand up, perked up at once.

Show off! I thought endearingly.

She shot me the sweetest smile and began to thump the table and babble louder and louder. I had never imagined I would find it in my heart to melt over a little child like this.

We ordered our drinks—her green apple soda and my Americano.

'Wanted to see you before I left.'

My heart sank. Though she looked like a blissed out, happy mother, somewhere in my heart I was so attracted to her that I had wanted to believe that she was a single mother. Why had she called to see me?

'Where you going?' I asked, retaining my calm.

'Prague.'

'Oh?'

'Was always fascinated by the sound of "Czechoslovakia". So...

'Hahaha,' I laughed, familiar with the little nuggets of humour her writing was peppered with.

The baby had walked up to me and was tapping my knee. Shyamli got up and scooped the baby in her arms. She wiped her drool with tissue, and when the baby protested angrily, scrunching her mouth into such a tight pinch that her chubby cheek puffed out,

Shyamli swung her high up in her arms, and the little one gurgled in delight. Motherhood suited her more than any other woman I'd seen. She did not look as young as she did back in the lobby days, but there was a certain serenity and joy radiating from her.

She put her face into the baby's belly and made a loud snorting noise. The baby threw its limbs about in glee. Then Shyamli hugged the baby so hard, it began to wriggle free. She kissed the baby's mouth, and I saw tears glint in her eyes.

My God! I would have thought a scene like this, in front of an almost stranger, a little melodramatic, but this seemed so natural. She set the kicking baby back on the floor beside the table and picked up her bag.

'Excuse me.'

I saw her turn into the narrow corridor that led to the washroom.

Suddenly, the baby lost her balance, and in a trice I was beside her, propping her up on her wobbly legs. I couldn't then resist picking her up in my arms. She looked at my face closely; then ran her grubby, drool-wet fingers on my stubbly cheek, landing it on my nose and tracing its shape in extreme concentration.

'Hello!'

Someone patted my shoulder from behind. I turned to find Sameer, my former colleague. 'Hey, you have a beautiful daughter. Congratulations, yaar! Where have you been hiding but? Someone said you were in London. Hey, she looks just like you. Look at those eyes. Exact same, man!'

Just like Samir, to bombard me with questions and not wait for a reply. I looked towards the washroom.

'Dude, I'm here for a client meeting. They are here. Catch you later?'

'Sure.' I wanted him to go before Shyamli returned. To avoid any explanation.

Shyamli was taking quite long. The baby was leaning out of my arms wanting to be set free on the floor again. I put her down by the table and put my arms to both her sides so she wouldn't fall and hurt herself. I didn't know I could feel this way for a baby. Perhaps, it is age. Mom and dad must be right about it being time for me to settle down. Imagine having one's own bundle of joy like this little munchkin. Imagine coming home to this one every evening; going to work with the stain of these wet fingers over my face. I was smiling.

There was still no trace of Shyamli. I turned to look. The washroom door was closed. Could she have locked herself in? I started to walk towards the washroom when the door suddenly opened, and some other woman stepped out. I looked around, then, walked up to the girl behind the counter.

'The child's mother, who just went into the washroom?'

'She left, Sir.'

My heart pounded against my ribs so hard, the sound reverberated in my ears. I rushed towards the door but was stopped by the baby's loud cry. Turning around, I saw her slumped on the floor. I ran and picked her up in my arms, trying to comfort her. Looking up, I saw Samir smiling at me from the far end. He gestured a thumbs up, lauding my fatherly skills, of course. That's when I saw a piece of paper on the seat where Shyamli had been sitting.

'Take the baby home, dear. Only you can do it. It belongs to your family.'

Holy Mother! This must be some mistake. Left holding a baby! People were staring at me. Dad! Dad would know. I called him. He didn't pick. Duh! His phone must be on silent. It was dad's nap hour. Oh Dad! What shall I do? Please, please wake up and tell me. What is this Shyamli has put me into? Dad, I've met her only a couple of times in the theatre. Okay, once when you were there—at the hotel. Yeah. I began to sweat.

That time, two years ago, when dad had come to Delhi to see me off to London, we were staying the night in a hotel. In the morning, I had gone out to meet my friends. My flight was late night and dad wanted to rest. I was to be back by evening, have dinner with him and then leave for the airport. But when I went to meet Atul for lunch, he got an urgent call and had to leave. Delhi was blazing, and I decided to return to the hotel and spend some time with dad instead.

It was almost four when I reached the hotel, and I was afraid to knock knowing it was dad's nap time. I lingered at the door and was about to walk away when I heard soft whispers. He seemed to be talking to someone, probably on the phone. I knocked.

When I entered, I found Shyamli sitting in a chair by the window with a cup of tea in her hand. She asked if I'd like some tea and proceeded to make me a cup, talking all the while. She said how she was visiting Delhi for a wedding and had casually called dad and what a coincidence it was that he too was here; so she made a dash for the hotel to meet him.

Dad was silent. He'd been silent for many days. I knew he was going to miss me. When Shyamli handed me the cup, I noticed that her hair was wet. Just washed. She looked beautiful—wet hair falling over her shoulder. But wet hair in Delhi's heat?

Dad was silent on the way to the airport. At the departure gate, he held me in a tight hug. I felt a terrible heaviness take over me then. Tears clouded my vision. We've always been close—dad and I. Everyone says I've taken after him in every way—our manner of speech, our love for theatre, our gait, our laugh. We have the same face, the same eyes.

The baby was growing restless in my arms.

Assorted voices, a broad sweep of imagination. This book is different.

How did this happen? When? Why was I kept in the dark? I, who was her editor for ten long years—not just an editor, we were friends.

We fought with each other over little things. 'Look Trisha, I'm not doing another line of this book if you don't accept this change. My reputation is on the line too, you know?' I would say.

There were long periods of sulking; not speaking with each other, and then she'd suddenly call to ask if I was up to going out for a play or lunch; or she'd ask some random question, 'Hey, if I use "wolf heart" do I necessary imply "cunning" as well?' She could have Googled. I would smile and come around.

Sometimes, I just wanted to stay miffed longer, and so I'd say, 'Why are you asking me? Google, no?

'Arre, tell me, are we not on speaking terms? I totally forgot.' Then she would begin her honey-entrapment, 'Oh why do you fight with me! It's so useless; I have so many things to ask. Now let it be, tell me about this wolf-heart thing.'

She had a wolf-heart too.

The Bog

A car had halted beside theirs at the signal. Ambika looked at its gleaming outline admiringly. The glass was tinted dark. Its long black body looking beautifully stretched out. As her gaze shifted to the window, she noticed a pair of eyes looking straight at her. Ambika looked away, embarrassed at being caught staring. But the eyes did not release their grip on her, and she was compelled to look again. A hand, a woman's delicate wrist was flung out of the hurriedly rolled down window. Before Ambika could react, the glass was as hurriedly rolled up. The traffic light turned green and the vehicles burst forth from the stop line in a mad frenzy. The black car zoomed past, as if on air.

'It sped, didn't it?' She turned to Alok.

'Idiots let loose!' Alok fumed as he negotiated the unruly traffic.

'I thought someone was looking out of that car. A woman.'

Alok didn't answer and let out an expletive as a biker cut him from the left.

'She looked terrified. I think she was trying to wave her hand out for help. Then someone just rolled the window up hurriedly.'

'What?'

'Do you think she was asking for help?' The unease she felt was growing by the minute.

After a few moments of silence, as they came out of the congested belly of the city and into the outskirts, Ambika turned to look at Alok and pleaded, 'Shouldn't we go after that car and find out? What if the poor girl is being kidnapped or raped inside the car or something?'

'Which car? For God's sake, Ambika! We can't go chasing cars on city roads just because you have an over-fertile imagination!'

He knew she would not be pacified, so bringing the car to the slow left lane, he reached out for her hand and squeezed it. 'It's nothing, darling. You are letting your imagination run.'

Mummy pushed her away. The way those words slithered viciously out of her mouth, through her lips, pressed together in disgust, Ambika felt the disgrace she was coiled in, tighten. She craved to be the achchi bacchi, but mummy was very angry.

It should never have happened.

The memory like a raw wound threatened to start pulsating again. Ambika stirred the dal and watched the fresh coriander, which she'd added too soon, wilt and turn grey, its flavour lost. The dal needed another boil for the right consistency, but she couldn't stand there watching it. It could become a green pond in no time. She shut her eyes. But even in the pitch dark, behind closed eyes, a purple patch began to glow and a hand emerged.

How could she run from something that was inside of her?

Turning the stove off, she stepped out into the balcony of their new apartment. 'Hello,' she said to the potted palm. 'I'm so happy to see you,' she said to the mogra buds, trying to superimpose the sound of her voice over the film that would otherwise begin to show in her head. The spotless, green potted plants stood pert in the places she had allotted them—neat little rows. All plastic.

Alok was waiting at the table for dinner. She set the bowl of dal before him and sat down. He kept watching TV, so she ladled the dal into a bowl for him. Without looking, he began to eat.

'The dal is different today…' he remarked with his mouth full. Was it a statement or a question?

'It's the same as every day,' she said, in defence. She had just realised that besides putting in the coriander early, she had forgotten to add tomatoes. The dal must be flavourless. She didn't take any. Alok was eating, unmindful again, lost in the news.They were now showing a black car that had been involved in a hit-and-run accident.

'Isn't this the same car?' Ambika stopped eating.

'Which?' Alok was filling his plate with too much bhindi fry.

'That car?'

The bhindi fry was chewy all of a sudden and Alok seemed to take his time controlling his rising temper.

With deliberate calm he started, 'There is absolutely no connection between the two. There are hundreds of such cars running on the roads; there are always hands, heads, and noses sticking out of car windows.' But he knew he had ended curtly, so he added, 'There is no need for you to waste any more thought on what you saw…or didn't.' He was firm.

She cleared the table and came to sit down next to him on the sofa where he had moved, still watching TV.

'I've lived in this city before,' Ambika said.

'Yesss!' Alok pumped his arm in the air, responding to a goal. Then suddenly becoming aware of something spoken to him, he went over the echo of her words hanging in the air between them, 'What?'

'I've lived here when I was very small.'

'Daddy didn't mention that when I told him we were moving.'

'We lived here when Tina died.'

'Oh.'

Later that night, sensing she was shutting herself in a silence, he attempted a truce. 'Have you been thinking of Tina? Do you want to talk about her, Ambi?'

'No,' she said and went into the bathroom. She took her time in there, but Alok was lying propped on his elbow waiting for her when she came back to bed.

'What happened? How did she die? Talk to me, Ambika. Don't let it eat into you like this.'

'Nothing is eating into me,' she switched off the light to close the conversation. Five minutes later, just as Alok began to doze off, he heard her voice in the darkness.

'Tina and I, we were best friends, we were like sisters. We wore each other's clothes; ate and bathed together; went to the same school, the same class; ate our tiffin together; sat together on the school bus.

'One day she asked me if I'd come to the pond at the edge of the colony. All kids had been instructed to stay away from that area. It was an open pond with nothing, not even a single brick wall to demark where safe ground ended and its pernicious periphery lay.

Even when we went past it with the elders, they tightened their holds on our hands. We threw in stones to watch the little splashes. The pond glugged up everything.

'Tina's uncle, visiting from Benaras, had gifted her a tin boat. It was a fascinating little toy because it wasn't a toy, it was the real thing. We poured in real kerosene and lit the small wick inside it, and just like a real steamboat it ran around in the tub of water Usha Aunty had placed for us to play in. But we were soon bored watching its rehearsed, limited runs. The idea of seeing it scuttle across the length of the green pond seized us. Nothing, other than the boat streaking across the wide pool, mattered to us; not even the thought of it not coming back into our hands again.

'So one afternoon, when our mothers and the maids were taking their nap, we both took off with the tin boat, a small medicine bottle full of kerosene, and a matchbox. We ran all the way to the pond. I still remember the frock I was wearing—a white polka dot with puffed sleeves, and Tina, her light blue polyester pants that mummy had got for me. Tina had thrown a tantrum asking Usha Aunty to get the very same for her, so mummy had given it to her without even bothering to tell me.

'We reached the pond and had a little tiff over who would fill the kerosene and who would light the match. She said the boat was hers, so she would allow only me to fill the kerosene. I was hurt by how she had said it, clutching the boat to her chest as she sat hunched on the grass, her blue polyester bell bottoms stretched on her knees, her feet dusty from the walk in the plastic chappals. Had it not been the excitement of handling the sharp-smelling kerosene, I would have snatched that boat from her and thrown it into the bog.

'After many failed attempts, she lit the wick and carefully began to walk towards the water. We realised that we could not reach the water without walking a little into the wet peat. We had never been so close to it before to know that the line of water would not be easily reached.

'"Don't be afraid, just follow me," Tina was confident as a grown up as she walked down the sloping side. I was scared, but I followed her. The ground felt soft. As we approached the blurred boundary of the water, our feet began to sink in. With every step, it was getting a little more difficult to pull our feet out and step ahead. My heart had begun to throb with misgiving. I knew we weren't doing right, but I couldn't admit it before she did.

'Everything happened in the blink of an eye, after that. Just as I realised that the distance between Tina and me had grown, she turned to look at me. I can see her now—her fear-smacked face. In an instant, I saw the boat fall from her hand into the muddy water. Its flame gave a sharp crackle and died. Tina was sliding away, the swamp sucking her into itself so quickly that already she was waist down in it.

'"Hold my hand, Ambi! Mummyyy." She held out her hand. Her scream rang out in the still afternoon, but there was no other human in sight. I looked on horrified. One foot in her direction and I was sinking too. I pulled myself away quickly. I climbed back and looking back was stunned to see just a hand.

'I only remember running back towards home and finding mummy and Usha Aunty, halfway, along with several people, come running towards me. "Where is my Teenu?" Aunty shook me by my shoulders and then without waiting for my answer, all of them ran towards the pond.

'Without food or comfort, my feet still caked in muck, I sat in my upstairs room hearing the ear-piercing wails all night. Everyone was crying, calling out to Tina, asking her to come back somehow, anyhow, begging forgiveness of God, promising to never scold her again, promising to be the best they could be to her, to love her like never before.

'Then daddy came for me. He hugged me so tight that I began to cry. He got me milk and bathed me with warm water in the dark night, rubbing my sore feet gently.

'When I woke up the next morning, I saw mummy come out of the bath. She seemed in a hurry, draping a white saree in the middle of the room. Her eyes were swollen, but her expression was strange—not sad, but kind of pinched. I got up quietly and went to her. I needed her to say something to me. She did not. So I went closer and hugged her over the half-done pleats of the white cotton saree.

'The shock of Tina was nothing compared to what came then. Mummy shook me off as she would an insect. I stood stunned, a little away, looking at her, waiting for her to realise her mistake and hold me back. Then I moved near her again. She looked into my eyes and said 'Aghori!'—and left.

'I was sent to nani in Ujjain. Six years later, when daddy got transferred to Ajmer, I went back to live with them. No one spoke of Tina or Usha Aunty ever again.'

Ambika was lying stiff. She wasn't crying anymore. Alok drew her close, 'Ambika, it wasn't your fault. You were a little child yourself.'

'But they never spoke about it. It made me wonder if they held it against me. If they thought I didn't help her; that I let her drown. I needed to talk about it. I needed to be told something. Why did everyone just block it out? She was my best friend. I missed her too.'

'It happens. They must have felt helpless too. It was a long time ago. You must try and forget it. Accidents happen all the time. You have no reason to feel guilty, because you did nothing wrong. Children do such pranks, unfortunately for you, it…went wrong.'

'That look in her eyes, the fear in her voice when she called out to me, "Hold my hand, Ambi"'. Ambika was taut with anguish. Gently, he stroked her back till she fell asleep.

Ambika began to withdraw into herself. She was given to melancholy, but this time it wasn't letting go of her. Grief spilled out of her heart and wreathed her in silence.

Ambika searched online maps for 'bog', 'swamp', 'pond', 'tank', 'lake', 'hole' even 'quagmire'. No results. The name of the colony, she did not remember.

What she did remember was a Christian cemetery at the far right of the bog on the dust track they took from their home—a shortcut to the market. When they went past it, grown-ups seemed to quicken their pace, especially after dark. She would crane her neck to see over the low boundary wall at the rectangular stone slabs, the crosses, and the rounded headstones and imagine people lying still beneath the stone, unable to breathe.

She googled it, located the market next to it, and one afternoon, took an auto to go there. The autowalla dropped her in front of a mall. This wasn't how she remembered the place—a tight clump of shops in a crescent, clenching a patch of green. There were no shops now, just the glass front of the mall.

Not knowing what else to do, she stepped inside. At the grocery store, walking the aisles, she tried to look engrossed in reading the fine print on labels of packaged pickles, jams, gravies, and sauces. Nothing she needed. Nothing she could use.

Picking up a pack of her favourite orange pekoe tea leaves, she stood in the long queue to bill. The brown paper package with the orange colour label justified this trip. She could now look for what she had come.

At the corner of the road, a cobbler in his shanty was driving small nails into the sole of a high-heel shoe. He looked up when her feet came to stop before him.

'Which is the way to the kabristaan?' She asked.

He pointed to his left, to a tarred bylane, closed in on both sides by multistoreyed apartment blocks that disappeared at a bend about 200 meters away. 'Shukriya,' she said and took the lane.

At the dead end, she noticed a dirt path next to a boundary wall. Looking over the wall, she saw the gate at the far end.

The gate used to be very big with a concrete arch over it, not a small, rickety one like this. It was quiet inside. She walked from grave to grave, reading out names—Prema Linda Abraham (nee Chacko), Mariyam Cunha, Natalia; Dear Baby, Lucy Pinto, Rose, Nisha…Beloved Wife, Beloved Daughter, Dearest Mother…

The sun was sinking swiftly behind the gulmohars rising above the west wall of the cemetery. The gulmohars seemed to breathe more heavily in the fading light. Looking up, she felt them closing down menacingly on her, as if they would scoop her up in their swaying branches any moment. She quickened her step towards the exit, suddenly realising that it seemed too far and too shrouded in darkness. Darkness began to descend all around her.

Someone jumped from the wall, landing right behind her. The lightness of a woman's body. Was a woman creeping up behind her? Terrified, she turned. A dried palm frond lay on the ground. She looked up at the tree and screamed. It was waving its arms, its long hair flying wild.

Ambika began to run but a hand gripped her left ankle. Not a strong grip but a cold, skeletal clench. Her scream died in her throat. She pulled her leg with all her might and managed to extricate her foot from the tight pincer grip. She turned to look. A dead branch, its dry shoots sticking out, lay on the path. That is when she saw the outline of the arch embedded into a high wall.

Ambika turned to a soft thud behind her and saw a corpse roll out of a grave. She stood rooted where she was as the corpse lay on her path. Slowly, it lifted its head. And spoke. She heard the words above her deafening heartbeat. 'I haven't eaten in many days, ma,' he begged.

Ambika lay awake thinking about the old cemetery arch, now walled in. So much had changed. As a child when she looked inside, the graves faced her; people under the stone slabs slept with their feet towards her. From where she entered this time, the tombstones lay with their backs to her. Her mind began to draw a map behind closed eyes—the big arched gate, the dust road that went past it, her house at one end and the market at the other. The bog across the road. Where was that road?

She broke out in cold sweat. The mall stood over the bog. A giant headstone for her friend.

Echo Point

The yellow was stretched to the horizon. Spring country. Millions of sunflowers held their satellite heads up, facing her. Walking up to the flowers, Smriti's heart throbbed in her ears—how to soak up such beauty? How to hold on to it?

'Arre Smriti, turn yaar.' She had barely turned when the camera clicked again. She wished she were alone. Turning around, she saw Shantanu gesturing to their cabbie, leaning on the bonnet of the car. The driver, his paunch jiggling ahead of him, came running down the slope and took the camera from him. Shantanu leapt beside her and put his arm around. His right hand landed on her left shoulder so heavily that she momentarily tilted away from him—a pose caught in their photos so often; it made her smile.

'Are we in the centre—where you see the cross? Okay then, click. Thank you.'

There would be hundreds of photos on the digital camera after the trip. Looking at the photos later, Smriti would feel a void in her memory from where she wanted to evoke the moment. The same flower or deer or mist-crowned hill, photographed over and over, so many times that even when she kept clicking forward while viewing them, the photos didn't seem to change.

'Your blue shirt looks good in pictures, but you have worn it too often.'...'I wish you had your glasses on in this one, you are squinting too much—that spoils the photo,' was all Shantanu would have to say.

'This is so beautiful. Can we stay for a bit?'

'Arre, there'll be more spots like this. We'll get down, pucca. Chalo now.' Shantanu was already walking towards the car.

Smriti looked at the sunflowers from the car window till the trail of yellow tapered away as the terrain rose. A blob of yellow on nature's colour palette—undiluted, pure. *What would you say, poet? Perhaps, you would quote Frost—a leaping tongue of bloom...*

The car wound up the steep hill road, washed clean by an early morning shower. The heat of the plains slid away, and as she rolled the window down, the cool breeze that blew in her face and hair, lifted her. Dawn flowers, their blue skirts full, festooned the tall oaks. Miniature paradises lay hidden among trees and turns. In the same scene she could catch a roaring waterfall, spurting out of the rocks on one side of the road, and a serene stream flowing languidly over its pebbled floor on the other. *What if I run into you here, poet? What if you were here too?*

As they climbed higher, the late afternoon shadows began to fill the valley below, with long strokes. Wisps of cloud and mist started to nestle between the folds of hills for the night. The driver halted at a bend. Many other vehicles were parked along the wide turn. She first heard it—the murmur of a waterfall. She could see from her seat excited, photo-clicking people. Shantanu had dozed off. She touched his arm lightly, but he did not wake. The cabbie had already stepped out and was stretching himself. Smriti got out of the car and gently pushed the door shut, careful not to make noise.

It seemed awkward to walk alone to the crowded lookout. *But you're with me.* Up closer, the fall was thunderous and splintered as it fell on rock shoulders, sending out sudden sprays on the onlookers, who ran in and out of the showers in glee, shouting and laughing. It touched her face and droplets shone on her hair as she walked to the edge of the ancient, bracken-covered culvert to look down at where the water crashed, hundreds of feet below. *Perhaps, you are somewhere among these crowds of people, standing quietly away, watching me.* She smiled and picked a fallen leaf to keep in her journal. *A memory of the moment.*

The journey had been tiring and Shantanu slept as soon as he hit the bed after a walk around the 'property' and a sumptuous, early dinner. *'Look thy last on all things lovely, every hour—let no night steal thy sense in deathly slumber...'* Smriti lay looking at the stars framed by her window even as the outside lights were switched off one by one, and the night sky presented itself in its absolute glory.

When she opened her eyes again, the sky was growing lighter. It wasn't daybreak yet, but there was light in the sky, and she could see mist rising in soft puffs. A bulbul, with its elegant crest and the hidden red jewel under its tail, hopped on the window ledge outside. Shantanu turned over. Smriti lay still waiting for his sleep to anchor again; then she quietly got out of bed. Pulling a woollen shawl over her nightdress, she stole out of the room.

There were no other early risers and the staff was not about yet. Her heart hummed. She walked to the edge of the lawn and looking at the town stretched out below, let the untouched air fill her. By and by, a spray of rouge appeared in the east. Some stray clouds caught the light of the rising sun still hidden from sight and glowed like embers in the sky. A row of silver oaks that lined the edge of the precipice, turned away from the breeze to reveal their silver undersides. Albino trees. *How would you describe this beauty, poet?*

'So, madam is here.' Shantanu dropped himself into a cane chair. The bulbul flew away. 'If your commune with nature is over, can we please have some tea?'

Smriti went inside.

Shantanu was on phone, talking to the reception when she came out of the bath later. 'That's fine, we'll cover these four points today and the other three tomorrow.' He kept the receiver down and said to her, 'Let's go for breakfast. We should leave by nine otherwise we won't be able to cover everything.'

'Shantanu, can't we just walk around today?'

'Where?'

'Where there are no people. Somewhere off the beaten path—'

'Meaning?' Annoyance singed his tone.

'I meant—these tourist spots are so boring. Same at every hill station—Sunrise Point, Sunset Point, Echo Point, Top Station—' Even as she said that, she knew she had spoken without caution.

'So why were you after my life to bring you to a hill station, baba?' To calm himself, he flapped his palms by the side of his head, as if he were stroking his invisible elephant ears. Then, very firmly, he stated, 'Now don't spoil the mood. We've come all the way, we must see everything. What's there in a walk? You do that back home every day, no? Look, I'm going to talk with the driver; you get dressed quickly and meet me at the dining hall for breakfast.'

Smriti left her hair wet and unbrushed as she came out of their room after him, and the breeze that blew through it, ruffled and set it wild. Shantanu was waiting at a table near the window that looked down at the town.

'Arre, what's this?'

'What?'

'Your hair! You haven't combed it?'

'I like it like this.'

'It'll look like a crow's nest in the photos.' His pursed his lips and twisted his mouth to one side, like he did to show displeasure.

They left to cover the spots marked out for the day. First, the coffee plantations. Getting down at tourist brochure specified spots, teeming with other tourists, they got themselves pictured with smiles, without smiles, with sunglasses, without sunglasses, with breeze in the hair, without…Smriti longed to walk through the endless labyrinths among the coffee shrubs, to get lost somewhere up there where the mist was caught and where the streams started. *Perhaps, you're waiting there, poet.*

'Oh flower garden! Stop, stop. Madam likes flowers,' Shantanu frightened the cabbie into suddenly stopping in the middle of the road as they drove to the next spot.

'No Shantanu, I don't want to go in there.' Smriti panicked when she caught sight of the long lines of people inside a public garden, walking from plant to plant, their faces set in obligatory admiration. Carefully cultivated blue roses, chocolate anthuriums, or powder-puff lilies bored her. She was weary of order and purpose.

'Come, we cannot not go!' Shantanu had already climbed out of the car and was holding the door open for her.

The 'flower show' was exquisite, the beds neat with no leaves astray, no stalks leaping out of the carefully pruned foliage to dance in the wind. Like contingents in a parade distinguished by their dress—the blues, the yellows, the mauves—they stood in formations, in apologetic pretence. Smriti longed for the clutch of black-eyed susans, they had driven past, growing by themselves in the wilderness.

'Chalo, now only Sunset Point is left for today. And Echo Point. We will go to Echo Point first. Anyway, Sunset Point will be nice only at sunset. Driver, take us to some restaurant for lunch and then to Echo Point.'

'Hellooo!' Shantanu called out, leaning precariously over the railing that overlooked a deep gorge. Nothing. The majestic hills that seemed to close in from all sides, even as they stood a hundred miles away, stared back silently. 'Hellooo,' he called out louder. The hills sent out a moan.

'Smriteeee,' his voice ripped and shattered the tranquillity of the surroundings. No sound returned that resembled her name.

'You try.'

'Noo…'

'Come yaar, this is fun. I could hear my voice come back.'

Smriti did not move closer to him where he stood on the yellow dot marked Echo Point. She leaned over the railing to look at the gorge below. The firs were blue in profusion. *Blue firs, green hills, oh poet, come! Look at this glorious beauty with me.*

Shantanu pulled her by the arm to the yellow spot.

'Call out my name now.'

Poet?—Let's soak in this bliss, this soothing silence, this splendour of the hills and the trees, this abyss full of wonder.

She looked at the scene in front. It was calling out to her with its silence, spurring her to lose herself into it, drown into its loveliness. One world before her—immense, eternal; another behind.

'Come on! Call out my name!' There was an edge to his voice that threatened to tear the canvas before her. She called out.

'Hemaaant!'

The Yellow Saree

'Where is Bro-co-li, didi?' someone behind me asked and touched my arm gently as I was picking the red Washingtons from the supermarket shelf.

'Hun?' I turned to ask. She was fourteenish, wearing a salwar kameez that was once got for a few thousands—a definite memsa'ab-hand-me-down, much like my own.

'Hari wali gobi? Green gobi,' she explained.

'Khatam, over,' I replied.

Smiling, she said, 'My madam will kill me.'

Long after she disappeared into the aisles, I thought about it. Her smile. The little crook!

How quickly we learn these survival tactics living in homes where we're smiled at and praised only in the presence of visitors; all the nice food gets over when it is time for us to eat; the memsa'ab comes with a kurta, 'Dekho, new kurta for you. *Very* expensive hai. Keep it for when I tell you to wear. You must be very grateful, even if you had chaffed your limbs off working, you would *never* have been able to wear such *grand* clothes,' and you smile and thank her and say it is 'bahoot beautiful' when you have just overheard her sister saying, 'Aise hi, lying about. I don't want this kachra. Give it to your girl, na.'

I'm preparing an army.

It began two years ago. After finishing the mopping in the fourth and last house, I was leaving, taking the garbage out, when Madam called out to me.

'That lady who does this stitching? What's her name? Take this blouse to her, one button has come off. And get it done today only. But first go drop that kachra, and wash your hands thoroughly. Don't dirty my blouse, okay? Bring it back tomorrow, *pucca!*'

On the way home, I stopped at Fatima's to give her the blouse. Her door was ajar and when I stepped inside, I found her lying on bed with high fever.

I came back home and got busy with the chores. Just before leaving for work the next morning, I remembered the blouse. A hook, it was. Dangling by a thin thread, like a child's milk tooth ready to fall. It required precisely four stitches. I do it all the time for my blouses. Funny that madam, who drives that shiny long car, who can shout at the traffic policeman and does the most beautiful icing on cakes, cannot put thread in a needle and stitch it back into place. The other day, when I was making the beds, she told me I never tuck the bedcover under the pillows properly. She showed it to me. 'Simple hai,' she said, 'It is not rocket science.' I hear it all the time—not rocket science. Maybe stitching buttons is rocket science.

If I took the blouse back to her, she would be upset and say, 'You are all the same. Always faking illness. What is a little fever? The thing is you all don't want to work. That is why you will never achieve anything in life. Like *this* only, you will clean and wash bartans in houses, till you die.'

How easily she says that. When she was forcing her sister to eat another piece of cake and the sister protested, 'I'll die!' Madam was so quick to shush her.

Anyway, I did not want any jhik-jhik, if I could help it. And help it, I could. So I took out my needle and thread, yanked the metal hook off the tiny thread it was hanging by and tucked it back firmly into her deep-neck blouse, the colour of a peacock's neck.

Madam didn't even look at it properly. She handed me a ten-rupee coin for Fatima.

The very next day, she gave me a yellow saree to get the fall done. Just as she handed it to me, and I started to tell her that Fatima was ill, her phone began to ring. 'I have no time to listen to your stories. Tell her to give it in two days and do a good job.' She turned to speak on the phone, 'Haiii jaan...'

I waited. The third house was locked when I had gone there earlier. I had to go back and check if they were back. I was hoping they were not. If I waited for madam's phone call to get over, I would get very late. So maybe, I thought, I'll just take it and tell her tomorrow that Fatima is ill and can't do it. Probably, Fatima would be well enough today to do it. So I left with the yellow saree.

The third house was still locked so I returned home early. On the way, I met Fatima's daughter, who told me that Fatima had jaundice and needed to rest for a long time.

I was looking forward to some relaxed time before the children returned from school. I ate my lunch of rice and dal while watching film songs on TV. I love film songs, and when no one is at home, I sing along.

The heroine was wearing a red saree and running on snow. The hero was wearing a red sweater. Some day, Radhe and I will also wear matching clothes, maybe when we go for a wedding.

The heroine was now in a white saree holding out the pallu. It was like a thin veil behind which her large breasts heaved in time with the beats of the song. The hero also wore a white shirt, and they ran into neat rows of flowers. When they came in yellow on the beach leaving perfect footprints on the sand, the hero splashed water on her and the heroine's saree stuck to her skin. I don't get to watch all this so peacefully with the children around.

The power went off. There was still one hour before the children returned, so I took out the yellow saree from the plastic bag madam gave it in. Taking off my saree, I draped the yellow saree. It felt like rui, cotton wool—light and soft—as if I wasn't wearing one. I looked into the small mirror and adjusted the pallu over my breasts like madam did—running it over the very tip of the right one and stretching it to the left shoulder. God! Everything inside could be seen.

I lifted my left arm and the pallu flowed like the heroine's. I waved it. Automatically, my feet rose, and I twirled on my toes, as if I were wearing shoes with heels. Humming the song I had just heard, I turned round and round, and danced, light and happy all of a sudden.

Just before the kids returned, I folded and kept the saree back into its cover. I could do the fall too, perhaps. I lifted the end of my saree to see how I had done. It looked okay; there were no creases.

So the next day, I went to the shop and bought the exact matching fall and thread and began to hem it on the saree. In no time, it was done. When I gave it to madam, she gave me fifty rupees. The fall had cost only ten.

When I did a fall for another of madam's friend, she remarked, 'Fatima's stitching has improved.'

So it began, and I was soon altering blouses and kurtas, hemming falls, and altering curtains. I bought a second-hand sewing machine on a monthly instalment.

The two neighbourhood girls—who were no good at school and had failed Class X twice; who would have been sucked into this work of making beds, cleaning toilets or playing ayahs—I got them to help me. I taught them to sew and even sent the brighter one to take stitching classes.

When Sakeena came to live in the neighbourhood, I discovered she could embroider. So we made tablecloths and napkins, like the ones I saw in the houses I mopped and dusted, and she adorned those with delicate patterns of leaves and flowers.

I still go to the houses, but now I do not mop and clean. I go to the supermarket to buy their soaps and creams, biscuits, and vegetables; I accompany their aged parents on walks in the sun and to banks or doctors' clinics; I sit outside the door when the

Math tutor comes to teach their girls—all things the memsa'abs can't find time for. My children say, I don't need to go to the houses at all. Just sit at home and supervise this work. But I need to go. It is to do what madam calls 'networking'. I have to keep the memsa'abs within my reach to get the work straight from their hands; I need them to see me to be reminded of that nice new saree that can perhaps, be stitched into a lehnga.

But they still don't know that there is no Fatima. Fatima died of her illness almost two years ago. If I tell them it is me who does their stitching, they may accuse me of deceiving them. They may never give me more work, and may even begin to look at my stitching with suspicion.

God bless the broccoli girl. Someday I will offer her a way out too. Then she will never again have to feign shame at being late to get the broccoli.

Did I say she 'had' a wolf-heart?!

There is a big news item in today's newspapers that the Vermont Arts Foundation has awarded its prestigious fellowship to the prolific Indian writer, Trisha Kumar. It includes a one-year residency and publication of her next book. There are glowing words for her body of work and the new collection of stories.

I'm glad for T.

Am I? Actually, I'm torn. Why did she do this to me? I cried after reading the review. Cried buckets. Cried buckets? I hate it when I use the expressions she used, when they stud themselves unbidden into my speech and writing like this. And into my memories. Memories are the hardest.

Those winter afternoons in my living room, when she'd be sprawled over the carpet, and over cups and cups of ginger tea, we'd go over the edits. She would say, 'Debika, people do this over mails! You make me sit here in front of you so you can get your way. I'm not doing another book with you ever!'

We did six books together. Six! By then we were conjoined twins in our heads—reading each other's thoughts and feelings. So during her 'dry days'—that's what she called the phase when she could not write—I'd ask when she started looking particularly run-down, taking care to not point to anything—home, relationships, finance or health issues—'Is all well otherwise?' And she would dismiss it with a vigour that seemed unnecessary.

'You know you can tell me,' I would persevere.

'I know, Debika. Will you teach me how to make amle ka murabba?' She'd say something so unrelated, not even using her brilliant mind to camouflage the fact that she was just trying to change the subject—pdq. That's her again, PDQ!

Sheela's Escape

Neatly peopled—one per seat—the chartered bus to ITO crossed the Yamuna Bridge, sped past Pragati Maidan and turned towards Connaught Place. The inside of the bus began to stir as it neared Gopaldas Towers, the first stop.

Sheela's hand moved to her shoulder for the habitual securing of dupatta and ensuring no straps showed. Clutching the handbag firmly under one arm, she climbed down the front exit. Her office was a short walk across the road. The bus had not moved, so she started to cross the road. The engine roared as she took a step forward, and she felt uncertain. The bus seemed tentative too—jerking back and forth, ready to start without warning.

It was too late to step back. She looked up, desperate to catch the driver's eye. Just as she reached his line of vision, he saw her and nodded. Relieved, she crossed. Once on the other side, Sheela turned. Her gaze followed the bus down the road as it turned right at the fire station. She saw the driver turn sideways to look at her and then the bus disappeared from sight. Sheela merged into the 9 am Connaught Place office crowd.

The next day, when Sheela got down at Gopaldas Towers, she waited for the bus to move on, so she could cross the road. But the bus didn't move. No one seemed to be getting down. She looked up and found the driver looking at her. With a flourish of his hand, he gestured her to cross and smiled courteously, waiting. A little flustered, Sheela gave a faint smile and looked away. She walked hurriedly across, aware of his eyes on her. Something trembled in her. It also put a smile on her lips for the rest of the day.

The life of Sheela Chaubey, 40, a teller at the Indian Bank, at the World Trade Centre, was decorously slotted—9 am to 5.30 pm, she was the diligent worker, helpful co-worker, and obliging subordinate; 6 pm to 7 pm, a bus commuter, like any other, to Yamuna-paar; 7 pm to 7.30 pm, a harried housewife, buying groceries and vegetables on her way home; and from 8 onwards the householder, cooking dinner, catching her favourite TV show or an occasional chat with a neighbour, the general doer of this and that till all her family returned home and ate. It was only by 11 that all that was required of her was done.

Until a few years back, Sheela had smiled at every customer at work and hummed songs while cooking. When and why she stopped went unnoticed. Perhaps, it was the daily commute across the grey, supine Yamuna, morning and evening. Perhaps, it was the limp hour at which she reached home. Perhaps, it was the fixity of Pitaji, sitting on the stone slab outside. She now lived without a smile or song. It simplified everything—living to go to work, to cook, and clean, to complete one task and move to the next.

Today her pace was brisk. She bought atta and walked past Pitaji, whose faraway look went through her as usual. She longed to lie down, watch TV, and have nothing to do. Prakash never returned home before nine; Pragati had the excuse of board exams to remain shut in her makeshift study area in the veranda, and Vikas would be at some street corner with other boys, scheming some mischief until dinner time.

She made some milky tea with extra sugar. Handing Pitaji some in a steel tumbler, she settled down in front of the TV. Film songs stirred her. Many years ago, she had imagined herself running through flower-filled fields, singing songs. Amitabh Bachchan in stylish pullovers and Rekha with lustrous lips were singing of love and longing, looking tenderly into each other's eyes.

Punita walked in. 'Pabiji, aj wade khush lag rahe ho! You are looking happy today.'

Some evenings when Sheela finished cooking dinner and Prakash was late, she stepped out to talk with Punita next door. They stood outside and talked until someone demanded something of them from either house.

'Pabiji, you toh at least go out na. My toh life goes in this chulla-chauka, the daily grind. God knows when I'll get rid of all this. Perhaps, now only in the next janam. I pray to God to not give such a life to anyone, not even to my worst dushman', Punita would often lament.

Sheela knew Punita would never understand the problems she faced in going out to work. Sometimes she wished she could just quit her job—just like that—stop going to work one morning. But she knew that they would never be able to make ends meet on Prakash's income alone. The whole day at the office and then all the housework. She was okay till Punita started to envy her.

'Pabiji, don't mind, but I think you should keep an eye on Pragati. She's growing up, and there is no one in the house all day to see where she goes and who she meets.'

'Kyon, what happened?'

'No, I saw her in the park yesterday—with a boy. First I thought it must be someone else. But you know, I could make out that pink kurta very clearly—remember that pink kurta that you and I bought together from that Kashmiri who came to our house? Oh, did I tell you that fellow came again some days back? He didn't have any variety only. I told him that you have sold off all the nice ones and have come to me with all the bacha-khucha leftovers that no one liked; so come back again when you have choice. And I also told him to come on a Sunday, so you too will be at home. I told him that this Pabiji goes to office and also has big girl so she might buy.'

'Achcha, but tell me about Pragati. Who was the boy? Are you sure it was her? He must be a classmate, they must be discussing something about school. Or, perhaps, it was Vikas?'

'Nah, nah, Pabiji, am I blind? You know these kids have grown up in front of my eyes. I know them too well.'

Later, as she sat watching TV, the children came too. Sheela kept eyeing Pragati. What if Pragati was involved with a boy? What if Pragati did not know right from wrong? What if Pragati did something wrong? Prakash would kill them both—mother and daughter. He would certainly make life impossible for Sheela. Already, there was little communication between them.

'Pragati, have you taken a kasam to not study? Are you going to sit in each class for two years like your bhai?' She threw a darting look at Vikas, who mumbled something like 'Not again!' and walked out of the house.

Sheela switched off the TV, and Pitaji, who was dozing off to the comforting hum of it, sat up. Pragati walked into the veranda slapping her slippers as loud as she could. Sheela hoped Prakash would return while she was holding up her foul mood.

She went into her room, the only bedroom in the house, and opened her trunk. She thought of the morning, and it made her smile. The lime green suit lay at the bottom. The last time she wore it, Misraji had commented, 'Aaj kuch khaas hai, something special.' Carefully, she ironed it on the bed and laid it out on top of the trunk to wear the next morning.

Eight fifteen, five minutes before her usual time, Sheela was at the bus stop. When she saw her bus coming, her heart began to throb. The suit seemed too conspicuous; the dressing up, too deliberate. But it was too late to do anything about it, so she put on a sullen look hoping it would balance it out. The driver wasn't looking her way. She got into her seat behind him.

For years she'd been travelling on the same bus. Same people, same seats, everyone knew everyone. After Sharmaji finished reading the front page of the *Hindustan Times*, he gave it to Mathur uncle. Sometimes the shy Abhijeet asked him for the sports page. The film-star type skinny girl, who never spoke, slept with her mouth open as soon as she got into her seat next to the door. Kalpana and Surbhi talked incessantly about home, family, food, shopping, and office. Sometimes Sheela joined in, but she preferred to look out of the window.

Now when she looked up, she saw the driver looking at her in his rear-view mirror. Warm blood rushed to her face when he smiled. Sheela gave a fleeting smile and quickly looked away. When her stop came, she got down, waited to gauge the driver's decision, found it favourable, crossed the road, and turned back to look at the bus. It became the moment of her day. The bus waited for her to cross the road each day.

Each day, she found herself thinking about the next morning—if she should look up and thank him, or smile; or if he would turn to look at her before the bus turned at the fire station.

Sheela began to sing again. She made pooris more often now, allowed Pragati to cut her hair and Vikas to grow his. She did the housework more earnestly and vigorously—Prakash's collars were scrubbed cleaner, the clothes were folded in neater piles, the utensils shone, and even the ash on the puja shelf was cleared every day. She never seemed to tire of housework. If everything was done for the day, she'd find something more to do. So at nine in the evening, she'd heat water in a big tub using the immersion rod and soak the curtains or sheets or bedcovers, then, sit scrubbing them late into the night.

A knot tightened in her stomach as the bus approach her stop, each morning. It made her feel young and special. But sometimes it made her anxious. Then she would take a different bus or, after getting down, walk right to the rear and cross the road from behind the bus, without even turning to look at the driver.

She didn't notice when Prakash started coming home later than usual. His name was Mahesh. The conductor called him 'Mahesh Bhai'. Did he know her name, she wondered. Prakash stopped chewing tulsi or pan masala before coming home. The smell of cheap liquor made her turn away from him and dream at the edge of the bed, reliving those few heady moments of the morning again and again.

The evening buses were more crowded, and the ladies preferred the front seat opposite the driver to being pressed against each other at the back. One evening, Sheela got in ahead of the others and sat down at the far end of the long seat, right in front. She felt eyes on her and looking up, found him at the wheel. She caught a surprised 'oh' escaping her lips, but her expression said it all. She was embarrassed. They were face to face for the first time.

Before she could react, Kalpana plonked herself next to her and seeing him, asked, 'Arre bhaiya, how come, this time?' He only smiled.

'Aap hi aaya karo, you are the best,' she carried on shamelessly. Kalpana could chat with anyone and so casually that no one really bothered about the appropriateness of her manner or what she said. Surbhi also joined them. Soon there were five women, squeezed into the long seat. Packed to capacity, the bus began to move.

Surbhi took out her knitting. 'Who is this for?' someone asked.

'Husband, who else,' Surbhi replied.

'Arre, it can be anyone. Not that your husband will come to know if you finish all the knitting in the bus.' Everyone guffawed.

'I wish!' Surbhi sighed dramatically. More laughter.

Krishna called out from the seat behind the driver's, 'Palak, where's my gajar halwa?'

'Oh, I forgot!' Palak took out a dabba—the halwa had been pressed and cut out into diamond-shaped burfees. It was passed around. They each took a piece.

Then Kalpana extended the dabba to the driver, 'Bhaiya, you also take. Yeh hamari Sheela, she makes the best gajar halwa in the world. One day she'll get it for us; won't you, Sheela?' Sheela turned red. But his smile was restrained and courteous.

That evening, for the first time, Sheela heard Pragati talking to him. A boy. She was whispering into the phone. Sheela let her be. Later that evening, when Pragati came to lie down beside her, Sheela moved closer and taking her head into her lap, she ran her fingers into Pragati's hair. 'Mera bachcha', she said and held her close.

One Monday morning, Reshma called out to Sheela from the second row across from her, 'Didi, how many chuttis do you have for Diwali?'

Reshma was seated at a distance and Sheela knew she would have to be loud. She also knew he was listening. Self-consciously, she replied, 'Thursday and Friday.'

'Oh, so four days. I have to come on Friday too. Lucky you all.' Reshma pulled a long face.

He came that Monday evening. He came again on Tuesday and on Wednesday evening. She felt he was doing it to make up for the coming holidays. On Wednesday, as the bus approached her stop, she was uneasy. What should she do? What should she say? She wasn't Kalpana to call out cheerily, 'Achcha bhaiya, Happy Diwali. Get Diwali mithai for us!' Sheela got down without a word. She turned back to look at him as the door shut after her.

Surrounded by family and chores during the Diwali weekend, Sheela found herself thinking more and more about him. On Diwali night, Prakash was brought home drunk by neighbours, who found him lying by the roadside. Sheela performed the puja with the two children and Pitaji dozing in his chair. Prakash's snores rose above their aarti.

Monday morning, Sheela was at the bus stop, eager for the brightness that had evaded her during the festival of lights. As the bus closed in, she strained her sight to check. It was another driver at the wheel. Incredulous, she stared at him, expecting him to at least explain, apologise for standing in for Mahesh. She got in and looked around at the other commuters, hoping she had got into a wrong bus, but Abhijeet caught her eye and greeted her, and Sharmaji and Mathur uncle were laughing at something.

She knew it. Men! He was deliberately doing this to her. He would laugh and feel very important when the conductor told him about her looking about anxiously. Immediately, she let her face fall back into a detached calmness she did not feel.

Tuesday. Again he didn't come. She decided that it was over; that she was never going to look for him again. She decided she didn't want to. She would change her timings. She would change her bus. Then again, why should she do all this for someone who meant nothing to her? He was just the driver who drove a public bus and she, just one of the passengers.

As she deliberated on this, a lingering anxiety about his well-being began to gnaw at her. What if he was ill? What if he's had an accident? She scanned local newspapers for bus accidents. There were none. Before long, the anger fizzled out and anxiety took over.

Sheela saw him as the bus approached her stop on Thursday morning. Her heart throbbed as she climbed in and immediately, before propriety could hold her impulse back, she asked, 'Aap aaye nahi? Where were you all these days?'

He smiled and answered, 'Ghar gaya tha, to my hometown in UP. How was your Diwali?' he asked.

They caught snatches of each other's lives, morning and evening—films, songs, titbits about fellow commuters, traffic jams, bus routes, and such.

When the first carrot of the season arrived, Sheela bought it at forty rupees a kilo to make halwa of two kilos of gajar and four kilos of milk. She added generous quantities of ghee and first packed a dabba before serving it to the family. While getting down at her stop next day, she left the dabba on the vacant seat next to the driver's. 'Someone left this here yesterday,' she said. He smiled and nodded.

The next morning, Sheela picked her empty dabba from her seat when she got in. She looked at him in the rear-view mirror. Mahesh smiled. She smiled back. That day the bus did not wait at Gopaldas Towers for Sheela Chaubey to get down and cross the road. It took a quick turn at the fire station and sped towards ITO to offload the last of its passengers. Sheela and Mahesh looked at each other in the rear-view mirror.

'Why are you in such a hurry always?' I'd ask her.

'My mind runs away with my thoughts. When I'm writing, my mind is like the mutual funds statuary warning.'

That quicksilver mind.

I should call her.

That day she got really drunk, she had said, 'Debika, I have only you. I don't have one person in the whole world who I can tell everything.'

'Come on, you have Shekhar.'

'I know,' she said, 'but you know how it is, husband is husband, one needs someone…else.'

Then quickly, she turned to the edits and moaned, 'Why have you changed this—"my bad"? That's how we speak!'

'Trisha, it's not sounding well; I thought "slip of tongue" is better.'

'And not "lapsus linguae"? Come on, Debika! Let's put the Wreninmartin aside.'

'Wren and Martin.'

Pushpa Aunty

'Don't try to dazzle me with your angrezi idiom! No one has two left feet. If you did, you'd have a birth deformity. Don't be such a pain.' Athira dragged me to the Zumba class.

Every day, at the cafe where we ate after work, women danced to peppy numbers at the fitness centre above. We were quite enthralled, but I kept making excuses to not join. Those flat-tummied, navel-pierced women in tank-tops, we sometimes bumped into while entering or leaving, seemed formidable.

'What will I wear?' I was hoping I'd found an excuse till the next shopping trip at least.

'You could spray paint yourself, if you like. Come on, who cares!' The two of us entered a room full of women of all ages, dressed, without discrimination, in bun-outlining leotards and neon tops. We got to the back of the class, trying to follow the moves of the girls in front. The next hour was as exhilarating as it was exhausting.

While leaving, I saw an older lady looking at me. She looked familiar, but I couldn't place her. She had been in the first row and I had watched her with admiration for her grace and fluidity of movements. I wished I saw her in regular clothes, so I could recognise if she was my dentist or someone I saw often at the grocery store. It was quite embarrassing to smile and not know.

In the next class, I stared at her more. I had reached early and found her sitting on the bench at the far end, reading a novel.

At 1.56 am my eyes flashed open. I had been thinking of home and her face loomed large.

She was not there in the next class on Tuesday. Was she avoiding me? Living incognito?

At the Thursday class I wasn't hoping to see her, but there she was, in an animal-print crop top, her hair in a high ponytail. She saw me enter and flashed a smile. After the class, when I saw her leaving in a hurry, I ran down the stairs after her.

'Excuse me?'

'Yes?' she turned to look straight at me.

'Are you…aren't you…?'

'Yes. Same. Good to see you, Bhoomi.' And she was gone.

'Uff! Two days into the class and madam is chasing hotties?' Ritu dropped herself into the chair beside me at the cafe.

I was laughing to myself. I decided not to tell Ritu about Pushpa Aunty.

We did not hear him open the gate and then the main door. Dad entered home while mummy and I were having an argument over a new pair of jeans I wanted. He was angry, 'You two can be heard in the street outside! For God's sake, put silencers in your throats, if you can't help fight like junglee womenfolk!'

He kept his bag on the table, where mummy absolutely detested seeing it, and continued, 'What will the neighbours say? Have you ever heard a sound from Pushpaji's house?'

Grrrr...I wanted to scratch that infuriating calm face of Pushpaji then!

Within a month of shifting into the neighbourhood, a small colony of office babus, many school teachers, and some class-two government officers, Pushpa had become the focus of everyone's attention. Although they were tenants, Pushpa's family had been elevated almost to the status of owners in the eyes of the neighbours because of the air of dignity with which she carried herself. The proverbial lady of the house, she kept a spick and span, well-managed and calm household. Like medals on her breast were her two grown-up children—a married daughter and a college-going son. To her middle-class neighbours, she and her husband had fulfilled their worldly responsibilities successfully by marrying off the daughter into a good family and had ensured a comfortable old age for themselves by investing well in the son's education so he would get a secure job.

Pushpa dispensed expert opinion on all and sundry—knitting patterns, preserving jams, maintaining black hair. She was always impeccably dressed in crisp cotton sarees and her hair was neatly tied in an elegant bun—a little higher than most housewives in the small-town locality would dare to sport. Her tall and luscious figure was secretly the object of envy for all—men and women alike.

Whenever Pushpa appeared at a gathering of ladies, an uncomfortable silence descended. They were obliged to put up an act when she was around. Nobody said things like, 'my husband threw off the thali last night because the roti was slightly burnt' or 'my mother-in-law is asking me to have another beta' in front of her. They tried to be like her—restrained and refined. Everyone was completely in awe of her.

Every morning at around eleven, Pushpa could be seen walking down the main street with magazines in her hand. Within an hour, she would return the same way, magazines in hand. If she saw someone outside their home, Pushpa would stop by to talk. The chit-chat would be restricted to 'Is lunch ready?' or 'Your saree is very pretty'—things that could be discussed standing on the street. If someone called her inside for a cup of tea, the conversation would go beyond this, and her advice would be sought on a variety of things. She would then come up with definitive statements, such as, 'You must put a lining on those dark curtains'; 'The proportion of amla in your henna seems to be more—your hair is brittle'.

Pushpa had two lovely grandchildren. More medallions. Whenever her daughter visited, Pushpa wasn't seen outside the house at all. With the added chores their visit would bring, the household would bustle with activity. She would only come out, when her husband left for office every morning. She would open the gate and wait there till her husband kick-started his scooter and drove past her and out of the gate. She'd close the gate after him, wait till he disappeared round the bend, then turn to go back inside.

The husband and the son did not mingle with the neighbours, but that too was seen as a sign of sobriety, and the 'reserved nature' was spoken of with admiration. Pushpa more than made up for them. It was a perfect family. No one heard a raised voice from their house. They never seemed to fight or disagree. No one ever seemed glum or angry or left home banging the door or leaving the gate unlatched. Theirs was a very respectable family.

I was in college in Delhi and visiting home during my winter vacations. We stayed two houses away from Pushpa's, and it irritated me no end to be compared with Pushpa Aunty always.

One afternoon, I was weeding the lawn with mummy when Pushpa Aunty walked past on her way back from the library. She saw us and stopped at the gate to talk. Reluctantly, I followed mummy to the gate to say hello, and as the two of them got talking, I returned to my work.

I found Pushpa Aunty's presence quite overbearing and wished that something or someone would shake off her propriety once and for all.

Later that day, over lunch, mummy mentioned that Pushpa Aunty wanted something to read as the library she went to every day was closed. Mummy had offered to lend her a novel, but Pushpa Aunty said her husband does not allow her to read novels.

'How ridiculous! How can a husband dictate such things? And Pushpa Aunty accepts such unreasonable control over her?' I was incredulous. Mummy shot a quick look at daddy, who looked as if he wanted to say something but did not. Mummy then glared at me—a warning to shut up.

But I was uneasy. It seemed unimaginable that a woman who seemed to have such immense power over the entire neighbourhood would bow down to such absurd restrictions in her private life.

Then on, I often thought about Pushpa Aunty. What is her real life like? What is she like behind her veil of decorum?

I returned to Delhi. That year my exams were delayed. Mummy had sent me a parcel with daddy's colleague. Along with the dabba of my favourite gajar halwa was her letter.

My Dear Mimi,

Hope your cold is better now. Take good care of yourself. How are your preparations for the exams going? Study hard, but do not overstrain yourself. Don't miss your morning and evening glass of milk. I wish I was with you now. But you know daddy's food has to be taken care of here.

We're okay. I'm making mango pickle. Bai had to go to her village, and I had to do everything myself—chopping, grinding, and mixing the masalas, then climbing up the terrace three times a day to sun it. Do let me know when the sweet chutney is over, I'll send some more if someone is going to Delhi.

Daddy is fine. Busy as usual. Yesterday, I'd gone for the Garden sarees exhibition with Mishra Aunty. I did not buy anything. Mishra Aunty got a hundred sarees opened and, then, she did not buy any. I felt so embarrassed.

Do you remember Pushpa Aunty who lived two houses away? You know what she did? Her son joined MBA course and went to live in a hostel. Soon after, as if she was only waiting for the opportunity, she too left. I've heard that she's living in a women's hostel. A married lady with grandchildren leaving her home and going and living in a hostel alone, imagine! Leaving her husband at this age. God knows, what else remains to be seen in this life.

Anyway, you don't bother about what's happening here. Concentrate on your studies. Best of luck.

Love,

Mummy

There are 15 stories in this collection! FIFTEEN I mean, I had no clue. She kept saying she was having a mountain of a writer's block and couldn't put finger to keyboard for one single word.

This was exactly one year ago.

Sometime in December last year, she had called and wept inconsolably on the phone. When I insisted she come over pronto, she said, she'd let me know. Then she sent me a WhatsApp message that said: it's just my PMS. No worries. But I promise, I'll see you soon.

I saw the message only late in the afternoon. All morning, I was fretting about her.

She could have called.

Lakshmi

After the customary forty-day rest, Lakshmi returned to the big bungalow where she cooked. The master of the house was a *big* government officer, who wore white clothes and was driven around in a big white car. The mistress was a tall, beautiful lady, who abhorred housework, especially cooking. Their two daughters were married into wealthy families and had moved to other cities—one to Gulbarga and the other to Pune. They were constantly in and out of their parents' home accompanied by a brood of boisterous kids.

The big bungalow had a sprawling lawn, flanked by fruit trees. A spacious verandah in the front was where the master met visitors. The inside of the house was cool and dark with a high ceiling and a long corridor that ran through it and opened at the other end into the inner courtyard.

The warm, tiled kitchen, the store next to it and the open washing area just outside the kitchen were Lakshmi's territory. Her mornings began with cleaning the utensils and the kitchen floor. After which she began the preparation for breakfast—boiling milk, cleaning and chopping vegetables. Though they themselves were frugal eaters, her employers had visitors on most days, and there was no time during the day when Lakshmi could turn the stove off. The years at the bungalow had made Lakshmi an expert cook. Everyone swore by her 'jasmine' idlis, her bisibele bhat, her mango rice, and the delectable jaggery-channa dal payasam. All day she cooked and cleaned. Some days, if lunch got over early, she took a few hours off to go home but returned in time to prepare the tiffin and dinner.

Since Venkatesh's birth, Prema, her eldest, had virtually taken over most of Lakshmi's household responsibilities. With Lakshmi returning to work, the roles had been reversed—Prema became a full-time mother to Venkatesh while Lakshmi managed the housework when she returned home. But the arrangement did not work beyond a couple of weeks, and the two younger daughters, Mamta and Kasturi, had to be sent off to Lakshmi's brother's house in the village. Prema with the baby Venkatesh began accompanying Lakshmi to work. She played with him in the courtyard all day. When he slept, she came in to help Lakshmi, or tired, she too dozed off next to him.

That winter Venkatesh was almost eight months old and had begun to crawl swiftly. At noon each day, the mistress came into the courtyard to sit in the sun. Venkatesh, despite Prema's strict vigilance, always seemed to find his way to the mistress.

One afternoon, he crawled up to her and began patting her knees and babbling. Prema went running after and picked him up, but he tugged at the mistress' saree and began wailing. The mistress admonished Prema asking her to let him be. Prema looked around nervously for her mother, then, set him back on the sun-warmed floor. Venkatesh scuttled back to the chair where the mistress was sitting and promptly began tapping her knee in glee. The mistress smiled at him.

As the babbling continued and grew louder, he began to dribble from one side of his mouth.

'Ai Prema, where are you? Go, get a cloth to clean his face,' the mistress called out.

Prema could not find a cloth. She usually used the end of her skirt for this purpose. So she picked Venkatesh and, turning away quickly, did just that—wiped his mouth with the end of her skirt.

'Chee!' the mistress got up in disgust. 'Lakshmi! Where are you? Come with me.' Lakshmi came rushing out of the kitchen wiping her hands on her saree. She followed the mistress back into the house.

The mistress led her into the storeroom, at the back of the master's bedroom and had her open the big tin trunk that contained old clothes. She began looking inside. There were baby clothes of her grandchildren that her daughters had dumped with her to 'give away to servants'. She rummaged through them and found some bibs and napkins with colourful cartoon characters. There was a lemon-coloured one with delicate white lace that Lakshmi remembered the master had brought from 'phoren'. The mistress smiled as she looked at and touched the clothes fondly. She neatly folded the lace-trimmed bib and kept it back into the trunk, while tossing several others to the floor. Lakshmi closed the trunk and picked the bibs from the floor for Venkatesh.

It became a ritual—every afternoon, when the mistress came out to sit in the sun, Venkatesh, with Mickey Mouse or Goofy around his neck, was released from Prema's hold to crawl up to the mistress and play around her. Just as lunch was over, Prema would give Venkatesh a quick clean up at the garden tap, wiping his face, hands, and legs with her skirt when no one was looking. Although

Prema and Lakshmi both felt proud and honoured by the privilege Venkatesh enjoyed, Prema had to stay alert and make sure that he did not annoy the mistress in any way. Secretly, she was happier without this added anxiety.

One day, inactivity, the sun's warmth, and her weariness made Prema doze off as she sat watching Venkatesh playing at the mistress' feet. The mistress looked towards the sleeping Prema, then stole a glance towards the kitchen door. Lakshmi too was not in sight. She extended her palm towards Venkatesh. Venkatesh grabbed it. The mistress smiled and softly called out his name.

'Venkatesh?' she touched his cheek lightly. He responded with a happy gurgle. Afraid it might draw Prema's attention, the mistress drew her hand back.

A few weeks later, the tin trunk in the storeroom was opened again, clothes rummaged through, and a pile of clothes, Venkatesh's size, selected. Barring the ones that looked very expensive or that had some sentiment attached, the rest were handed over to Lakshmi with the strict instruction to always have Venkatesh dressed in them. The clothes were to be washed and kept clean at all times, the mistress had instructed.

So, by the time he was one and a half years old, Venkatesh had begun to be dressed up like the babalogs. And it was now not unusual to find him sitting on the mistress' lap, playing with her gold chain or bangles.

There was a puja in the house that morning, and the daughters were visiting with their families. By four in the afternoon, just when Lakshmi finished washing the utensils, the children came asking for something to eat.

The mistress called from her bedroom, 'Lakshmi, give them milk first, then make something to eat.' As Lakshmi kept the milk on the stove to warm, the children saw Venkatesh entering the kitchen from the back door. They began teasing him. He hid behind his mother's saree. Lakshmi handed the children each a glass of milk. Venkatesh looked up at her and gestured towards the glasses. She called out to Prema to take him away, but Venkatesh began to wail. His crying brought the mistress to the kitchen. She poured out some milk—not a full glass, just three fourths, and not with Bournvita, like the rest—and handed it to Venkatesh. He gulped it down with relish.

'Do you keep him hungry all day, Lakshmi?' the mistress asked her. 'From tomorrow, let him have half a glass of milk in the evening.'

Mamta and Kasturi returned home when Venkatesh was two. Prema stopped accompanying Lakshmi to the bungalow to be with her sisters at home. Venkatesh did not require constant care now and was left playing by himself. Lakshmi kept an eye on him and attended to his needs between her kitchen duties. More often than not, just when she was caught up with something urgent, he would demand her attention. And at such times, the mistress would magically appear and carry him away. He now had access to the mistress' bedroom where she left him playing on the floor beside her bed.

One day, when the master was away and the mistress was having lunch alone while watching TV, Venkatesh walked up to her. She smiled and fed him some rice and curd she was finishing off her meal with. He demanded more, so she called out to Lakshmi for a fresh plateful of rice and curd. Had the mistress implied in some way that the food was for Venkatesh, Lakshmi would have taken him away on some pretext. But she had just been asked for more rice and curd.

Lakshmi watched from the doorway as the mistress scooped up a handful of rice and took it to Venkatesh's mouth. Slipping it into his mouth, her fingers touched his mouth in a very intimate way. It made Lakshmi flare up with anger to see her son so eager; she wanted to slap him. The mistress, oblivious to the pair of eyes staring at the scene from behind, continued to gather the rice in her fingers and feed him. Lakshmi returned to the kitchen.

The next morning, for the first time in eleven years, Lakshmi did not feel like going to the big bungalow. For eleven years it had been so much a part of her routine that she had seldom stopped to think about it. She was irritated because she could not come up with an excuse to stay back and finally, got up to go. Venkatesh, like every day, came after her. She pulled her saree away from his grip and pushed him inside, calling out to Prema to shut the door. Venkatesh's wails went with her.

She was late by an hour. As she entered from the back door, she could see the mistress in the kitchen. She quickly went to the handpump in the courtyard to wash her hands and feet before entering the kitchen. The mistress turned around angrily at the sound of the handpump. 'Is this the time to come? Do you expect me to do all your work? The master is waiting for breakfast. You people have no sense of time. The more we do for you, the more you all want. If you cannot take care of this work, let me know, I'll find someone else,' she gave her an earful. Lakshmi kept quiet.

The mistress looked about Lakshmi. Lakshmi knew but did not offer any explanation.

'You came alone today?'

'Yes.'

'Oh, do what you like! You people are thankless,' she banged the large brinjal she was holding on the floor and disappeared into the house.

In the afternoon, the mistress walked into the kitchen again.

The frown marks were still threateningly etched on her forehead like a warning for Lakshmi.

'Why were you late in the morning?' The control in her voice was palpable.

'I had a headache.'

'Did you take medicine?'

'No, it has gone now.'

'Hmm…I could not find the big knife today. Where did you keep it?'

'It's here.'

'Hmm…'

'So where did you leave Venkatesh?'

'With Prema.'

'Is he unwell?'

'No.

'Now onwards, come on time.' And she walked out.

In a couple of months, the routine was set for Lakshmi. She went to the bungalow in the morning with Venkatesh. He was almost three now. He played inside the house, in the mistress' room, watched TV, had all meals with her, and generally clung to her all day. The mistress started buying clothes and toys for him.

One afternoon, Lakshmi was busy in the kitchen preparing jackfruit pachadi. The previous evening, the master on seeing the jackfruit being brought in from the garden had laughingly commented, knowing Lakshmi was within earshot, 'So will we get to taste jackfruit pachadi this year or not?'

Lakshmi had squeezed herself behind the kitchen door shyly because even this little reference to her cooking was an acknowledgement of her efforts. The master had a weakness for sweets, but for the past one year, since he had been diagnosed with diabetes, sweets had been totally banned at home. Recently, the mistress had told her that his sugar was okay, so Lakshmi was permitted to add jaggery or cook something sweet once a week.

After lunch each day, when the master retired for his afternoon siesta, the house fell into a hush. Lakshmi too stole a quick nap sometimes. At other times, she prepared the four-o'clock tiffin and the dinner at a relaxed pace, engrossed in her thoughts. If she ventured out of the kitchen, she could sometimes hear Venkatesh's squeals from the mistress' room. Since the days were hot, they had begun to spend the afternoons indoors.

In one clean thrust of the sharpest knife, she cut the jackfruit open at the centre. The resin oozed out and began to tie the knife and her fingers in sticky threads. Soon, she would need to marry off Prema. There was no money. Her brother had asked for Prema's hand for his eldest son. The mistress had told her that marriages among first cousins were not good. The children born of such marriages will have serious physical and mental defects. Dipping her fingers into the bowl of mustard oil and then spattering the knife liberally with more, she started peeling off its porcupine skin. The insides were creamy white.

She remembered how one seller at the vegetable market last evening had rejoiced when he cut open a jackfruit and found it tender and white inside. Ecstatic, he called out to customers, 'Look, it's butter!' People thronged to buy chunks. He was asking Rs 20 per kg. She had twenty in all and had to buy vegetables to last at least three days.

She cut the peeled half into four smaller pieces and began chopping them into fine shreds. Perhaps, the mistress would ask her to take a small part of the fruit—from near the stem, as she sometimes did. Then she could make the spicy curry for the kids. It would have to be watery for the jackfruit would not be enough for so many mouths, but she always managed by adding more red chillies and, sometimes, potatoes to make the gravy thicker.

The smell of pure, homemade ghee wafted through the kitchen as she heated it in the wok and added the shredded jackfruit. A cloud of steam went up with a swish when she poured water into it and covered the wok.

She had tried to tell the mistress that she had no dowry to pay. Also, in their community, a brother helped to lessen the sister's load by way of offering his son for his sister's daughters. But the mistress had walked out of the kitchen saying, 'Do what you like. But I'm telling you, you will regret this decision one day.'

She added the jaggery and waited for it to come to a boil. Removing the wok from the stove, she prepared the tempering with mustard seeds. Not sure if she should make it spicy by adding green chillies or leave it sweet and add some cardamom instead, she thought it better to ask the mistress, who was likely to get upset if it was not what she expected. So Lakshmi tiptoed to the mistress' room. The door was slightly ajar, and she could hear the mistress talking softly to Venkatesh.

She looked around and then pressed her face close to the door, peering in. The mistress was holding Venkatesh tightly on her lap and kissing him repeatedly, all the while coaxing him to call her amma.

Call me amma,' she kissed him. 'Always call me amma, okay?' 'Who's your amma, tell?' Venkatesh shyly pointed towards her. 'No, don't show, call.' He called out, eyes shining with mischief, as if in a secret game, 'Ammmma!' She pressed him to her bosom and kissed him again.

Lakshmi returned to the kitchen. She added the green chillies to the pachadi.

The grey clouds were bunching up above as they did at noontime every day. Lakshmi sat under the mango tree peeling the shallots for the sambar and thinking about Prema. Why was her brother not fixing the match? Why had he not spoken? Already she had seen in the eyes of her nephew, Santosh, a certain fondness for Mamta who though younger than Prema, looked fuller and was the prettiest of her girls. If she waited another year or two, she was afraid that not only Santosh but also her own brother might have a preference for Mamta, over the skinny Prema.

'So Lakshmi, what have you decided about Venkatesh's school?' The mistress had come out to pick a towel from the clothesline. She had stopped being indirect and took all decisions regarding Venkatesh, only making a pretence of asking or involving Lakshmi.

'When he is five, he will go to the government school where his sisters study.'

'That place! And why so late? This is the right time to put him in school. If you cannot do anything about it, let me know. I'll get him admitted to Nursery class now.'

'We cannot pay for private school.' Lakshmi too did not mince her words.

'Uff! Who's asking you to pay? You are hell-bent on spoiling his life. Okay, you don't worry. I'll pay for his schooling. Tomorrow, I'll take him there. Be here with him at eight in the morning, sharp.' And she walked away.

Sharp. The word reverberated unpleasantly.

'And don't forget to give him a good scrub in the morning,' she called out from inside before vanishing behind the closed doors of her bedroom where Venkatesh was sleeping—on her bed, his hands stretched above his head—happy abandon in sleep as in waking; and his mouth peacefully, contentedly, half open.

Lakshmi felt a sudden rush of maternal affection. She wanted to go and gather his soft, plump form into her arms and just hold him close to her heart. Her son. But she knew better. The shallots were bringing tears to her eyes.

The next day, Venkatesh was taken in the car to his new school. He sat beside the mistress in the back seat. Lakshmi was not asked to come along. So while she washed and cleaned and prepared food, Venkatesh, her son, was admitted to a private school in the posh neighbourhood. He came back with a new school bag, tiffin box, and water bottle. While leaving that evening, Lakshmi hid those in the storeroom. She did not want the girls, who carried their torn and discoloured bags to school year after year, to see these.

After school Venkatesh would come straight to the bungalow, have lunch and sleep in the mistress' bedroom. When he got up, Lakshmi would be called out to get milk for him. Then, as Lakshmi completed her work, he sat reciting poems in English to the mistress. The mistress laughed and sang with him, sometimes clapping her hands and raising her knees that Lakshmi found unbecoming of her.

When it was time to leave for home, Venkatesh would throw a tantrum. He would refuse to go with Lakshmi and hide behind the mistress. The mistress would initially make a pretence of being aloof and uninvolved, but when Lakshmi tried to pry him away from her, she would get angry.

One day, Venkatesh began crying, and the mistress snapped at Lakshmi, 'Let him be. Leave him here tonight.' Then a little softly, 'What difference does it make to you?'

What should she do? She thought. She took a small ball of rice-flour dough and placed it on the hot oil in the middle of the searing pan. Moistening her fingers with a little water, she gently pressed the dough and added a handful of chopped onions and green chillies over the biscuit-size roti, pressing it again. They needed this money. Where else could she go? Start sweeping and cleaning other people's toilets? What would happen to the girls? She dipped her fingers in water and pressed the roti again.

The mistress' sister was visiting from Bombay. She was there only for a day, and all her choicest food had been laid out. Who would cook all this in Bombay? There was no time, she had repeated so many times.

Lakshmi made one hole in the centre of the roti with her forefinger. Imagine! He stayed back here! She made some more holes. No attachment with mother or sisters. What did I not do for him? But he's a baby. What would he understand? Mistress should understand. Why, she has her grandchildren! Lakshmi poured ghee over the roti—a little more than she would have normally done. Putting a lid over the akki roti, she reduced the flame. The mistress' sister had brought Lakshmi a green saree.

Now the mistress had begun to detain her in the evenings with some last minute chore. By the time she finished, Venkatesh would be dozing, and she would look at him lovingly and say to Lakshmi, 'Why do you want to wake him up? Anyway he will only sleep, na—here or there it's the same.' Then quickly add, 'It's your decision. Do what you like.' Lakshmi would walk back home alone.

It was the day after Makar Sankranti. The master was rushed to the hospital in the early hours. By 6 am, he had breathed his last. Gloom descended upon the house. It was filled with mourners. The mistress sat on the floor in the hall, next to the master's body not speaking and refusing even water to drink.

For several days she sat like this. When people went up to her and expressed their sorrow and reminded her of the master's gentle and generous ways, she would weep. The daughters came with their families and wept, hugging their mother. Relatives from other towns came and cursed the city traffic and complained about mosquitoes that did not allow them to sleep.

Lakshmi did not go home for four days. She cooked and cleaned and did all the other odd jobs that were to be done. All this while, Venkatesh remained with the mistress; sitting on her lap. When on the fourth evening, Lakshmi went to ask the mistress for leave to go home for the night, the mistress nodded, but at the same time her hold on Venkatesh's arms seemed to tighten as he sat playing with a toy car. Lakshmi did not ask.

One year went by. Venkatesh never returned home. Babu had started staying drunk all day. He had been thrown out of his job. He abused and hit Lakshmi almost every day. In his drunken state, he constantly asked her where *his* son was. He even accused her of having sold him for money to the rich people in the big bungalow.

One day, he followed Lakshmi to the bungalow. As she entered from the back door, she turned to look. He had stopped on the road some distance away but was now walking to the front of the bungalow. She murmured a prayer, 'Om Shri Venkatesh Prabhu, let the mistress not see him. Please let him go back home and not say anything to her. I will offer you a coconut in the evening, if he goes away without creating drama.'

Lord Venkatesh was offered a coconut that evening.

Over the next one year, one by one, all the servants left. All those who had stood before the master with their heads bent and palms folded, spoke only when spoken to, now found other jobs. All self-seeking, shameful people, with no regard for the mistress, Lakshmi thought.

First to go was the guard. How, for the past so many years, he had rushed to open the gates and raised his right hand to his forehead in salaam every time the master drove past in his white office car. So pleased he seemed doing that, he carried the smile long afterwards. The gardener just stopped coming. His absence was not felt because he had stopped caring for the garden much earlier. The big trees were braving it, but the smaller plants were now dry stalks that stuck out like needles in the parched garden.

Then one day, the mistress asked the washerwoman to come only once a week to wash the 'big' clothes. She added with a soft sigh, which only Lakshmi heard that 'there are only her clothes now, which she can wash herself.' The next day, when Lakshmi went to get a bucket from the mistress' bathroom she found her clothes soaking in a bucket. She sat down and washed the clothes. From then on, the clothes were left soaking in the bucket every day.

The daughters' visits also grew less frequent. Initially, they took turns to visit their mother each month. But gradually, the complaints started growing: 'Going anywhere by auto is so tough'; 'The children get very bored here'—all because the official car was not there to run them to beauty parlours and shopping malls and the kids to cinemas and amusement parks.

The elder one started one day, 'Amma, why did you stop the washerwoman? See, such a load of unwashed clothes I'll have to carry back with me.' Then perhaps, realising that she was being rude, 'No Amma, I'm saying it for you. You should buy a washing machine now if that Sushila is acting smart.'

The younger one was more finicky about the house, 'Amma, you should change the curtains. And look at this carpet! It's gone, can't you see!' Lakshmi fumed as she watched the mistress' helplessness even as she replied to her daughters with patience and always managed a 'will do it soon.'

Lakshmi was sure it wasn't her imagination that the moment the daughters left, the mistress seemed to relax. But like any other mother, she would soon begin to wait for their phone calls and visits. They called often. And sometimes also asked for Lakshmi and told her to look after their mother well.

Lakshmi did her best to return the favours of the master and the mistress for the years she had been with them, but her own domestic problems were steadily growing. With Babu's salary gone, Lakshmi now more than ever, felt the burden of caring for her family, of feeding her three daughters. Her brother had still not formalised the marriage proposal for Prema though their mother, who seemed to be counting her final days had expressed it as her last wish.

Lakshmi's routine had been reset. She left early for the bungalow. While she prepared sandwiches with tomato and cheese for Venkatesh's yellow Mickey Mouse tiffin box, the mistress bathed him. With hot water. In her bathroom. Once, Lakshmi had been summoned to the mistress' bedroom to look for Venkatesh's school badge and was, unwittingly, witness to the morning ritual.

Venkatesh, with beads of water hanging from the ends of his dark curls, was running on the bed, and the mistress was after him with a towel. He was giggling, and the mistress was chiding him in mock anger. Then she caught him and wrapped his damp body in the big towel. Flowers, the size of her palms clung around his body. She patted him dry and gave his wet hair a nice rub.

Lakshmi looked away shyly from the naked body of her son exposed to the mistress like this. The mistress held up his underwear before him and he, holding on to her shoulders, slipped his legs into it. She daubed fragrant talcum powder on his neck, under his arms and then helped him into his uniform. Holding his cheeks in a firm pinch of her thumb and forefinger, she parted his hair and combed it neatly down his ears, all the while his mouth pried open like that of a fish.

When he came out of the room, he looked every inch like the other kids in the neighbourhood. But Lakshmi only felt anger towards him. Who did he think he was? She wanted to give him one tight slap and drag him home never to return. Instead, she watched from the door as Venkatesh stood holding the mistress' hand while they waited for the school bus.

When he got into the big yellow bus, he quickly rushed to a window and sticking his tiny face out waved to the mistress, whose continuous 'bye-bye' was drowned by the roar of the bus engine.

When Venkatesh returned from school at one, the mistress fed him hot rice and ghee. Afternoons were quiet, and Lakshmi often got a couple of hours to herself as she waited for the mistress to come out of her room after her siesta. Then she served her and Venkatesh tea and tiffin. Tiffin was less elaborate than when the master was around. On most days, the mistress desired only some biscuits. Six was usually when Lakshmi finished making dinner and left—dinner for two.

She covered the way back home faster as she did not have to keep pace with Venkatesh anymore.

Status Quo

I close my eyes. The bottle gourd in my hands feels like the calf of her leg. Firm flesh. I strain to summon up more of her, but the smooth skin I touch lacks the warmth of her pulsating life.

The first time I ran my fingers over her back, I was stuck by its softness. Like her moods, her body changed avatars. Sometimes, a bird, vulnerable, wanting to be held close in my embrace, to be protected; at others, playful like a pup, sitting on my lap one moment and teasing me, running away, the other, all the while talking incessantly.

She thought I didn't know why she talked non-stop. It was her anxiety about us—where we were headed, if we were, or if we would remain thus. 'Status quo', she said with a disturbing smile and cut it short. She didn't want our conversation to veer into that. At times she was full of desire like a mogra bud, ready to unfold, burst open. Her body stretched willingly to release and curl itself around my desire. Coiled together we lay for such endless moments. I thought we would begin to grow into each other.

Her calves. She moved around the house during her impromptu trips to the city, completely at home in her well-worn tie-dye top and denim three fourths.

'What do you call it?' I asked her once. 'One third?'

She laughed, 'Chef ji, how do you manage? Such an awful sense of proportion!'

Under the frayed ends of the blue denim, her calves showed taut as she walked—like the tightness of skin over just-ripe tomatoes. I drop the knife over half-chopped tomatoes for the pasta arrabbiata she loves and rush after her to scoop her in my arms.

'What?' She laughs. And when she lies on her back, I watch her legs. There is this dent on her shin, as if she had walked into something while her flesh was fresh cement, impressionable. I see my love as a two-year-old running blindly around her home in baby-glee, dashing her shin against the low edge of something—a divan, a trunk, a low table, or a large vessel. Ouch!

I kiss the dent. Tickled, she draws her leg up. I watch her eyes glisten; the hint of a dimple on her left cheek shyly deepens. Why can't you feel my love? Why can't you take it? Why do you always find it less? I wonder as she lies, sunning her honey-glazed body.

The late afternoon winter sun from the western windows warms her back while the white ribbed Panipat bedcover imprints its pattern onto her front. Like a gulabjamun soaking up the golden syrup—for me, for later. It dilutes my anger, my disappointments. It diluted her too.

She called often. To fight; to cry. I saw her less. I don't know why. We talked on phone. There were long periods of no fights, just love—nothing more, nothing less. Love talk. Once, overwhelmed, when all of a sudden I said that I'd come to her soon, she dismissed it by talking of other things. It angered me. For the longest time, we only texted. She wrote about long hours outside doctors' waiting rooms and investigations, followed by stretched silences as she swam and sank on the waves of drugged wooziness.

It began to eat her. Gnaw at her flesh and mind alike. She said it was my love. The last time she came, there was less of her. The new building, in the west, blocked the winter sunlight on the bed where she sat; her body bare, her thoughts elsewhere. I lay next to her, full of remorse, and counted the ribs down her spine. The dimple on the lower back was lost. She turned to me. The smile was smaller now. 'My little girl, my baby.' I held her close. 'I will
care for you and nurse you to health,' I promised. 'We must spend more time together.' I heated mustard oil and rubbed it over her soft back. My fingers ran over the knots of her pain. I could see the effort she was making to keep her eyes from closing. I sponged her back with warm water.

'Jaan?'

'Yes?'

'Nothing,' she smiled contently.

One day she called, 'I'm wearing the green dress you got me. Remember, I wore it to your show?'

'Yes, where are you going?'

'Nowhere. Just. Jaan, I tried to make your spinach-paneer sandwich. I'm almost there.' She laughed—a laboured laugh.

She had sat on the kitchen counter nibbling the sandwich I

made her that cold November afternoon. She was swinging her legs, totally engrossed in the eating. I got tea for myself and stood leaning against the counter facing her, watching. She looked up and smiled. Then, plucked out a plump piece of paneer from the sandwich and reached out for my mouth.

'I can't find that invite!' She was frantic over the phone.

'Which, my love?'

'The invite for your launch.'

'I haven't sent it to you yet.'

'Nooo, that one, last November. You had written on the back. Oh, I have to find it!'

'Come on! I'll give you another.'

'NO! You don't understand! I need that one. It had that moment.'

Why do you cling to stuff, my love, when I am all yours? But I didn't say that to her. I didn't say anything ever. She needed my words. My word.

She sat on my lap in the old rocker, her cold nose touching my left earlobe lightly; she twined my janeau around her finger. 'Daddy wore one too.'

'Daddy's girl! You need a daddy.'

'Will you be him?'

'Always.'

She let her head rest on my heart.

She's in the hospital, a friend called. I wanted to talk, but they said she could not. I flew. I prayed. She was a little mass under the sheet with tubes running out of her body, her little bird life attached to beeping, flickering machines. I called out to her, I begged, I cried, but she did not move, nor open her eyes. The waiting people, the nurses, the doctors, looked at me helplessly, with empathy in their eyes.

I wanted to give her so much. I thought, I would.

'Let's just cuddle,' she'd say. 'Let's just be friends,' then looking at my quizzical expression, 'Very good friends. I love you the most, the mostest. But don't touch me now. I want to feel your love. Tell me you love me, sitting over there,' she'd point to the chair away from her. 'Tell me you love me when I am away. Not away-away, but in the next room. Are you warm in the thought of it? Can you lie beside me and just hold hands?'

I couldn't let that soft mouth of her talk like that. I had to make it stop. She would protest. I wouldn't let her.

That day when I woke up to find her rummaging through her bag, it wasn't morning yet, and I was loath to wake up. But when she looked up at me, her eyes were pink as roses and the cheeks burned when I touched her. She took out some meds, gulped them without water, and lay down, turned away from me. The fever abated. But she threw up whatever she ate, and so we were at the doctor's clinic.

I watched her sitting on the cold steel chair of the waiting room and drinking water from a bottle. As she lifted her head up to drink, some of it dribbled down her chin and into her grey tee. She lowered her head again and sat with the bottle between her knees. One drop of water sat on her lower lip. It hung from its succulent redness like dew. And for several selfish moments, all I wanted was to take her home, to have her to myself.

She had looked up then and said with her eyes. That's what she had said a lot, always wistfully, 'I know what you want.'

A doctor gently placed her hand on my shoulder.

'Are you—a relative?

When she had first started her 'I-will-never-be-able-to-write-again' tirade two years ago, I would chide her and tell her to stop stressing. I told her to go on a holiday.

'Will you come with me? Let's do a girlie trip. Let's go to a beach and drink all day—'gham galat,' isn't that what they say?'

'Silly girl! Go with Shekhar. Go to the mountains. Soak in the fresh air, walk, and eat.'

'Hmm.' she said and abruptly, 'Hey, I've to answer the door. Catch you!'

City Girl

She pulled the dohar over her head, but the ringing of the phone muffled through it relentless. Reluctantly, she drew it back a chink and opening one eye glanced at the bedside clock—6.30 am.

Pankaj's parents were on phone from Ludhiana. It was her fifth wedding anniversary. Pankaj, who was travelling, had made the customary midnight call. Mummyji completed the usual 'putrawati ho, saubhagyawati ho, phoolo-phalo'. Each blessing seemed to taunt Rhea. However well she prepared herself for it, those words never failed to enrage her.

'May you be the mother of sons, may your husband, your suhaag, my son live long…' Why does she never bless me directly, without linking me to her son?

Mother-in-law continued, 'What did the doctor say? Are you following her advice? Are you eating proper food? Office jobs can be strenuous, take leave and relax at home. I toh always tell you, there's no need for you to work only. By the grace of God, my Pankaj earns so well.'

How about asking your son to stay with me? Perhaps, that would get you a grandchild? Rhea swallowed her indignation and got out of bed.

Determined to not let it spoil her mood, she thought of the day ahead—she needed to get her head around the new project timeline. Quickly, she made herself some coffee, checked her mails, and then stepped into the shower. Standing under the warm water, she let her body, rigid with resentment, relax.

Dressing up never failed to cheer her up, so she took her time drying her hair and rubbing her favourite body butter into her moist skin. Reaching out for clothes, Rhea's eyes sought the new turquoise shirt, which though she had not saved for the occasion, she felt like wearing. She needed all the self-love today. Indulgently, she painted her nails to match the pink matte of her lipstick. Usually, if she was alone at home, she did not bother with the breakfast, just had a fruit and some cereal in cold milk, but today she cooked for herself—scrambled eggs, fried tomatoes, toast, and coffee.

The greetings were waiting on the whiteboard at her workstation. She strained to read the signatures—almost fifteen of them squeezed into the tiny space. Colleagues who shared her bay, Lakshmi, Malini, and Sandeep had got her flowers—a large bouquet of turquoise orchids. She caught Simi's eye. Simi winked. 'Very pretty,' she murmured amid the demands for a treat. As soon as the bustle died, Rhea went down two floors from her fifteenth-floor office to where some of the team sat. Tim wasn't in his seat. It was almost ten, and she was deep into the discussion with the other designer, Rakesh, when he walked in.

'Morning!' His greeting was brisk, but she caught him looking at her and thought he was going to say something but he didn't. He picked up the draft of timelines and allocations she had left on his desk and, without looking up at her again, said in a low, sarcastic tone, 'Amazing.'

She smiled to herself secretly, a little thrilled to have stumped him thus. Timelines were meant to be unrealistic.

'I'll get back to you on this,' he said, waving the papers in his hand.

'Sure,' she said and left.

The blue orchids. Rhea looked at them with compassion. A few days back, she was having coffee with Simi at the Barista near office when they saw someone carrying a bunch of those turquoise orchids. Curious, Rhea dragged Simi to the florists next door. Sure enough, a big bucket of turquoise orchids was prominently on display. Rhea picked up a stalk. A small plastic tube filled with blue liquid hung from it. Repulsed, she asked the florist, 'What is this?' pointing at the coloured water.

'Madam, we make them here only. We have more, see.' He pulled out some green and purple gladioli from other buckets, beaming with pride at his ingenuity.

'This is horrid!' Rhea whispered to Simi and pulled her out of the shop.

The doctor had drawn up a new fertility 'plan'. She had prescribed new oral meds. This current gynec was among the many she had seen over the last two years to help her conceive. Her in-laws had chosen the doctor. The best in Bangalore—they had told Rhea. This was after they had tried all kinds of herbs, charms, and bribes to gods.

Rhea had to visit the gynec every month. The gynec would prescribe a medicine and declare, 'This will definitely do it.' Despite that, Rhea would get her period. The gynec would then proclaim, 'This is *veeerry* unusual. It has never failed. Okay, now this one I'm going to give you is absolutely sure-shot.' But Rhea would be back at the clinic the next month, sitting in the sterile, solemn waiting room, leafing through *5 ways to get pregnant faster; 8 ways to boost your fertility; ovulation calculator; what's your baby-making IQ...*

At a point during meditation, she often felt her 'self' leave her body and rise above it like steam. In mid-air, she turned like a skewer and looked down on her body. A shell. Nothing more. She tried to summon the same detachment as she lay on the examination table, without her clothes.

Because she was a 'complex' case, there was always a group of interns and junior doctors standing around the table to watch. Without being asked, she would remove her trousers and her panties and pulling her shirt up, lie there for them to examine her intimate anatomical parts, waiting for the visit to get over.

During all this, Pankaj had never accompanied her. Initially, the gynec had asked for the husband, then she too had stopped.

Rhea ran a finger over a smooth blue petal. She could see its intricate pattern of blue veins. Counterfeit blue. The medicines must run like a dye in her body. Rhea realised she had missed the morning dose. 'That's it then, I stop from today.' She suddenly felt very determined and strong. She was with a secret.

After work, she took her team for drinks and dinner. Tim excused himself as he had other commitments. She tried speaking with Pankaj on the way back home, but he did not pick his phone. Perhaps, he'd put it on silent and forgotten, she told herself. She texted him and went to bed.

Two weeks later, Rhea was having lunch in the office cafeteria, which, as always, was overfull. As soon as two people sharing her table got up, Bala came with his lunch tray. With him was Tim.

'May we?' asked Bala and sat down as soon as she nodded, since her mouth was full.

Tim sat across from her. He was engrossed in his meal and hardly looked up. He did sneer when their conversation turned to Hindi movies.

'I loved the locale in that one. I would love to go there sometime.' Rhea became wistful. 'I'm accumulating my leave for a long holiday. I want to see the Northeast, the Andamans, Kerala—' letting off a quiet sigh, she added, 'But my husband has no time.'

'So you go,' Tim sneered, still not looking up.

'I can't go alone.'

He sniggered again, offending Rhea. The group that was sitting on their long table finished eating and left and another set of people took their places. The clamour in the dining hall went up many decibels with the pushing and pulling of chairs, setting down of steel trays and glasses on the steel tables, and lunching people's voices.

Tim spoke, his voice cutting through the din straight to her, only for her ears, 'I'm going to my hometown in Kerala this week. If you like, you can come with me. That is, if you don't have a problem getting *permission?*' His eyes bored into hers, like he was trying to read something. 'You can tell me by tomorrow morning. I have to book the tickets. Excuse me.' He picked his tray and was gone.

Was that a challenge? Was he mocking her married status and her limitations? Putting her guts to test? But what an offer! A dream she wouldn't dare dream with eyes open. Yet, how could she go? What would she tell Pankaj? Need she tell Pankaj at all? She could say she was going with a girlfriend? What if he found out? And Tim? Would he think less of her for jumping to his offer so eagerly?

'Simi, would you have gone?'

'Where?'

'Kerala. With Tim?'

'Hey, serious? Isn't Pankaj in town?

Rhea shook her head, 'Won't be back till next weekend.'

'Tell you what? Go!' Simi winked. 'I see no harm.'

'I badly need a break,' Rhea tried to justify.

'Go then! Why worry? It's your life.'

Simi pulled up her chair closer. 'What's the big deal? Get a life, girl. Do what your heart tells you. Just be discreet. Really, Rhea, don't let marriage stifle you like this.'

Rhea sat looking at the worksheets open before her with vacant eyes. She needed to decide. At six, she went down to Tim's workstation.

'Not leaving yet?'

'Yep, right away,' He picked his helmet in one hand and his jacket in the other. Just as he mumbled, 'Catch you, tomorrow,' she said, 'I'm also coming.'

'Good.'

'Downstairs.' She specified.

'Okay.'

Inside the lift, she waited for him to ask, but he remained silent.

'About the Kerala trip, were you serious?'

'I'm never *not* serious, girl.'

'Yeah, but you haven't told me the details—how you are going? For how long? Where in Kerala?'

'I'm off for about five days. Our home is in the Waynad district.'

'You have work there?'

'There's some work at our tea gardens. Free otherwise.'

'You think I'll…'

'I can show you around a bit. But it isn't really a touristy place. There are no backwaters or anything. A small town, simple life. And you can stay with my family.'

'Thanks, but I can stay in a hotel. Nice of you to offer. But I haven't decided to go yet,' she added quickly.

Silence.

'Who all are there at your place?'

'Only my parents. Though lots of others—extended family—uncles, aunts, cousins stay around. You'll be safe.'

'Arre, I was just asking!'

'So you're coming. I'll book the tickets tomorrow morning.' He made way for her to step out of the lift.

'I do want to see Kerala, but I'm not sure. In the sense…you know?' She looked at him to see if he understood but was met with a quick blank stare. 'Do you think it's okay?' Then, afraid he might say 'no', she added, 'I hope it's not a bother?' As they walked across the lobby, she had to run to keep pace with his long strides.

'Women! It's decided now, okay?'

'Okay,' she waited, but he did not say more, waved his hand and turned to the stairway going down to the basement parking.

At night when Pankaj called, Rhea had already rehearsed her lines several times. She told him she needed a break, and since Lakshmi was travelling to Kerala, she had decided to go with her. The tickets had already been booked as it had to be done today.

'You okay with it? I know, I should have asked…but it all happened in such a hurry. Anyway, if you want me to not go, I can always get my ticket cancelled. I thought this break would do me good. You're also not home before next week.' She left no scope for him to say no without sounding uncaring.

But it angered her so much that she had to take his 'permission'—like Tim had said. What is my life come to?

Just before leaving on Friday evening, she called her mother. When she heard of Rhea's plan of visiting Kerala with a friend, mummy sounded happy for her. 'Mummy, why do I have to ask Pankaj for everything—take his permission? He just informs me of his plans.'

'We cannot live like islands in a family, beti. It's good you ask him. He should too, but don't worry too much about things you cannot change. Now run, it's time already, and be safe and happy.' Rhea kept the phone down and wept. Only mummy seemed to understand, but she too wanted her to adjust.

At ten thirty they stood on platform number three, next to his small and her large bag. She liked to carry enough clothes and footwear to have something appropriate to wear always. Besides, this was for five days.

'Tim, you didn't tell me about the hotels there? You know, I'll feel like an intruder—I mean…'

'Hey, stop worrying. You're my charge now. Just leave everything to me.'

'Have you told your parents that I'm coming with you?'

'It's home! What did that poet of yours say? Home is a place where when you go, they have to take you in…something?'

He remembered Frost!

They had some sugary tea to kill time. Soon the train pulled in. Tim picked up both their bags and led her to her berth. Their berths weren't together.

'My seat is further up. Will you be okay by yourself? It's just a matter of a few hours. I don't like to ask for unnecessary favours,' he looked around and said.

'No worries. I'll be fine,' she didn't show her disappointment.

He nodded and walked away. She saw his tall frame disappear and then turned her attention to the others around her.

A family of three—father, mother, and daughter—who had set up a temporary home in the train. The man had changed into a lungi and was shaking one folded knee, vigorously. The girl and the mother talked to each other in whispers and giggled. The string of jasmine in the mother's hair scented the whole coupe.

There were two other girls, who were together. One was skinny with large dancer-eyes, wearing aqua blue nail paint and a nose ring; the other, with her hair cropped short was wearing a collared shirt and lace-up boots. They sat close together. After a bit, the skinny girl put her arm through the other girl's and rested her head on her shoulder. Perhaps, they were sisters or best friends.

Rhea lay on her berth, too excited to sleep. As soon as the lights were turned off, both the girls climbed up on the side berth above hers. It was two, when the skinny girl climbed down. She straightened her kurta and stood looking up, right next to Rhea, where her thigh touched Rhea's foot. The other girl bent down and they kissed—a long passionate kiss in the dark passage.

Rhea forced her eyes shut, pretending to be asleep and withdrew her foot where it was touching the girl. She realised she wasn't just embarrassed to be caught staring at two people in an intimate act, she was repulsed. Why was she repulsed? Why was she judging them? What about herself? Was what she felt for Tim, acceptable?

I am just going on a trip with a colleague, she told herself. But she knew better—a male colleague she was awfully attracted to. Rhea brushed aside the unsettling thoughts. She was living a dream and decided she would not hold it against the lesbian couple.

In the bus, their seats were together. It was four in the morning, but Rhea couldn't be wider awake. 'You know Tim, this is high adventure for me. I've never travelled on my own. Imagine, going to Kerala like this!'

'Don't go with too many expectations, you may be disappointed. Like I told you, it's not a touristy place. But it's very beautiful.' She noticed a hint of a smile, some pride as he said that.

The bus started an hour late, and as they turned westward, the road ahead shone like a stream of gold with the first rays from the east falling on it.

'Sultan Bhatheri' the signboards on the closed shops read.

Kerala. The town was astir. The men in white mundus, holding both ends in their hands, as if to gather wind and set sail; the taut-skinned women, their long hair, oiled and loosely tied; kids with even, white teeth—everyone and everything appeared scrubbed clean. Soon they were in the open countryside again with tea gardens on both sides like carpets of green hung out to dry.

A milestone read 'Kalpetta 2 km'.

'Tim, I think we're there,' she touched him lightly on his arm. Tim stretched himself and walked up to the driver to ask him to stop the bus near his home.

They got down and stood watching the bus grow small and disappear on the endless road into the horizon. Rhea felt the crisp air tinged with the warmth of the morning sun caress her skin.

'We've to walk a short distance. You okay?'

'Absolutely.'

Tim carried both their bags across the road. Just as they crossed, she saw a middle-aged man come running towards them. He spoke excitedly in Malayalam with Tim and took the bags from him. It was the first time she was hearing Tim talk in Malayalam. The man nodded at her and carrying both bags on his head almost ran ahead of them, leading the way.

They turned right into a bylane and came upon a small gate that opened to a flight of steps, leading to a beautiful peach coloured, double-storey bungalow. This was the side entrance to the house with pink lace curtains fluttering in the open windows. A large terrace on the first floor overlooked the lawn where a middle-aged couple sat in cane chairs. They got up to their feet when the travellers appeared at the top of the stairs.

Tim's dad was tall and well-built and, like everyone else she'd seen till then, wore a white mundu and shirt. His mother's oval face was calm, and her cheeks rose into perfect rounds when she smiled. She hugged Tim and smiled at Rhea. Tim said something in Malayalam, and she frowned.

'I told mom you want to stay in a hotel. Stay here, she insists.'

Rhea smiled, 'Thanks. That's very nice of you. I hope it is not too much of a bother.'

'Not at all, it's our pleasure. Timothy's friends are like our children.' His father's English had a strong Malayalam lilt. Rhea smiled. They kept talking. She only understood his name being taken. Timothy. How nice.

'Will you have coffee first, or shall I show you your room?' Tim asked.

'I'd like to freshen up first, please,' she said.

Tim led her through the hall, up the stairs to the rightmost corner room. He held the door open as she stepped in. It was a small but longish room with windows on the entire east and south walls. The eastern side let in the beautiful morning sun as Tim pulled the drapes away. It looked down at a kitchen patch and the tea gardens formed a lush backdrop. She could see tall, windmill-like coconut trees, everywhere.

'This is amazing. I could just stay inside this room and be happy for the rest of my life!' Tim smiled. 'I'll see you for coffee...tea,' he said and left.

When she went downstairs later, they were having coffee on the lawn. She took in the refreshing morning breeze and waited to be asked. Tim sensed her thoughts and said, 'Thambi is getting tea for you.' She was soon handed a cup of sweet, milky tea.

'So, where does your husband work?' his dad enquired. Tim has filled them in, she thought.

'He's with a finance company.'

'You should bring him along next time.' He added courteously.

'That is very kind of you. Thank you.'

Rhea had mixed feelings about the mention of husband. But at least they would not harbour any suspicion about her relationship with Tim…Timothy. They were just friends. Tim was different at home. He smiled more, sniggered less. And he looked at her more.

After a nice, warm bath, she changed into a white cotton salwar-kameez. People in Kerala seemed to like white clothes. She put on her pearl earrings and went down for breakfast.

Just as his mother passed her the platters of piping hot idiyappams and vegetable stew, Tim came down the stairs looking relaxed in a tee and shorts. He ate ravenously without talking much. Rhea and his father carried on the little conversation that took place. His mother kept smiling at her from across the table. When coffee came, Tim asked her, 'Would you rather have tea?'

'Coffee is fine, thank you.'

His mother spoke to him. 'Mom is asking what you'd like for lunch.'

'Anything, I'm not very particular.'

'Okay, then I'll ask her to make both fish and mutton.'

Rhea smiled, 'I love curd rice.'

'And sambar?'

He remembered.

'Please don't put aunty to any inconvenience because of me.' Rhea spoke to him, looking at his mother, a little confused about how to talk with her directly.

'Relax, this is home. She'll be very happy to cook nine types of vegetables for you.'

Soon after breakfast, Tim and his father disappeared into the study. Rhea called up Pankaj to tell him that she'd reached safely.

He asked if the 'accommodation' was okay, and she said it was great. There was no mention of a hotel or of Lakshmi's home or anything. Pankaj was busy. It saved her the bother of supplying details and feeling guilty about the lies.

Tim's mother came to sit with her in the garden. She spoke in a curious mix of Malayalam, English, gestures, and very compelling facial expressions. She asked why Rhea was not wearing gold bangles. Then she looked for a gold chain, which too was missing. She looked at her hair and said 'oil' and 'black'. Rhea wondered if she thought her blond highlights were a result of poor health. Then came the overhanging, all-important question, 'Marriage, when?' When Rhea told her, she counted the five years on her fingers and asked, 'No issue?' Then she crossed herself and muttered a prayer.

Rhea went up to her room to fetch the box of mithai and a crystal vase she'd bought for them. Tim's mother placed the vase in the glass showcase in the front room and stuffed some blue plastic flowers that she pulled out from another brass vase that had stood there. She then went into the kitchen to supervise lunch. Rhea sat in the lawn leafing through a magazine and dozed off. She woke up as a shadow fell on her.

'Rip Van Winkle, time for lunch.'

Tim continued to stand between her and the sun. He looked straight down at her, a little amused. 'You take a nap in the afternoon, after that I'll take you around. No nightlife. But once my cousins come to know I'm here, there won't be any peace.'

The delicious sambar with rice and the vegetables in coconut gravy, plus the warm breeze that smelt of trees, lulled Rhea to sleep on the bed against the open window that brought in the chatter and clinking of vessels from the kitchen below. She woke up at the sound of knocking on her door. Thambi brought in tea and biscuits. He pointed to the door and said, 'Sunset.'

Rhea found Tim on the porch next to a Royal Enfield. With the lid of the oil tank in his hand, he was shaking the bike to gauge how much oil there was in the tank. 'Come on,' he said, and as soon as she got on, he zoomed on to the highway, where their morning bus had vanished. On the way, several people smiled and nodded at him. Perhaps, he too smiled back. Rhea held on to her flying hair, her dupatta, her kurta. The ground rose sharply. When they got down, Tim turned to look at her wind-blown hair, watering eyes, and smiled.

'Why tourist, where's your camera?'

She had decided not to bring a camera along. Memories were enough. They watched the sun go down and sat in silence on a big rock as shadows gathered around them.

'Wanna come for a ride through the wildlife sanctuary?'

'Is it safe? I mean, at this hour...on a bike?'

'Safer than me.'

The road was wide and ran through the forest. All around them shadows were congealing quickly. The air was still with only the rustling of leaves and the hum of life settling in them for the night. Rhea was relieved they did not spot any animals. She would have been very scared. Tim kept talking, telling her about the forest and his various encounters with wildlife. She hung on to his every word, trying to remember the details, to make memories. She did not want this ride to end.

Malayalam mixed with laughter reached them as Tim brought the bike to a halt on the porch.

'Great! The clan is here,' he smiled at her and pushed open the door, whispering into her ear, 'This can be wilder than outside.' As she entered the hall, full of people, everyone stopped talking and looked at her. Suddenly, she felt very conscious. What was she doing here in the midst of strangers? Not one person knew her—

not even the person she'd come so far with. When they finished shaking hands and hugging Tim, all eyes again came to rest on her—the stranger in the room. Tim introduced her to Uncle Jacob, his daughters Sara and Marina, Uncle Joseph's son Sam and Sam's friend Pete. There was a short lull from the awkwardness a family feels in the presence of an outsider.

When everyone was seated again, the conversation sputtered as everyone tried to speak in English even as Malayalam flowed. Rhea smiled so they would know she did not mind. It was a merry gathering. Uncle Jacob had a loud laugh. Sara was pleasant; her long hair was fashionably straightened. Marina was very tall with high cheekbones—like a model. Both were casually, but elegantly dressed. Sam could not speak without getting excited. Pete, the friend, was the stunner with tender eyes and spoke only when spoken to.

The boys were going to a bachelors' night and Tim was dragged along. Before leaving, Tim came to her and whispered, his face so close to hers that she worried others would notice, 'Don't hesitate to ask mom if you need anything. I'll be late. Sleep tight.'

After the boys left, the older people became engrossed in their talk and Rhea was left to the girls. They asked her a hundred questions about herself and about Tim—their work and their life in Bangalore. She wondered what they thought of her, of them together.

The night spread out a sequined sky before her as she lay on the bed, sleepless. The sky seemed so much closer than it did back home. She wondered when she had last stayed up looking at the sky like this and fell asleep trying to hear the sound of Tim's return.

Tim absented himself from the morning tea, then breakfast too. After breakfast, Tim's parents went off to visit someone and Rhea walked around the garden. It was ten thirty and still no sign of Tim. All she could hear was the wind in the trees and the sound of leaves falling, occasionally, a sound from the house as the servants carried out the chores. God, what will I not give for an idyllic life like this! She slumped on a chair and closed her eyes to the soothing sunshine.

She was wearing a pink Lucknawi kameez, it made her blush to think of that day in office when she was late for the Monday morning meeting. As she entered the meeting room, everyone's eyes were on her. Her manager, the cunning Fleur, lifted her eyes from the status report she was reading and exclaimed, 'Such a pretty picture you make in pink, Rhea.' Rhea knew it was meant to convey that her late entry had been noticed. But Fleur had more on her mind, turning to the rest, she continued, 'Doesn't she? What Tim?' Rhea was taken aback. It felt like she had been exposed, her secret made public.

Later that day, when Tim came to her bay to set up a programme on her computer, Lakshmi teased him, 'What Tim, you didn't say in the morning. Tell us. She looks like a rosebud, no?' Without looking up from the computer screen, he replied, 'Pink's not my favourite colour, but it looks nice on her.'

Tim was sitting right across her when she opened her eyes. He looked up from the newspaper he was reading. She did not speak. She could ask how the party was, what time he returned, tell him that she lay awake for a long time and that she waited for him at breakfast, but nothing seemed more meaningful than this silence that had placed them together in a haven where nothing could invade their silent communion.

They sat like that till his mother came. She wanted to make palak paneer because she said Tim loved it. She asked Rhea for the recipe. Tim tried to be the interpreter but gave up saying, 'Why don't you just show her?' It seemed like a good idea. So off the women went into the kitchen. Tim called after them, 'After lunch, I'll take you around.'

'This is Pookot Lake.' Rhea stood hypnotised by the placid pool surrounded by lush vegetation; the profusion of violet water lilies that clung to the edge of the water like a necklace of amethysts.

'This is the quieter part. There is a more touristy side out there,' Tim pointed. 'Boats and all. And there's an aquarium too. You wanna go there?' She shook her head and sat down on a stone. The beauty of her surroundings was so overwhelming; she felt the sound of her own voice might break the spell. Tim walked away towards the lake. She watched his silhouette. The late afternoon light fell on the rippling waters gleaming silver and it was like Tim had been placed in a picture.

That evening after dinner, Rhea and Tim walked barefoot on the grass and talked about work for the first time. Rhea asked, 'Do you miss home in Bangalore?'

'If I hadn't gone away, I wouldn't know what all this means to me. I enjoy both lives. And I'm lucky I have both.'

'Hmm...'

'You are a city girl.'

'Yeah, I've never lived anywhere else. Living here is so different... so dreamlike.'

'It can be a challenge.' He continued, 'Like if you are used to city life, when you want to do stuff that's only possible in big cities, then the conflict starts.'

She wondered about his conflicts.

'My parents say they're proud of my career. My father keeps me involved in all his estate matters. He's very passionate about this land and this life. I'm doing what I wanted to, what I studied for, but I know that one day I will be pulled back here. I'll come back happily. A farmer.'

'That's nice.'

'What? A farmer?'

'Yeah, and also to know what one really wants. To be so sure.'

'I love this life, lived close to nature, working with hands, physical work. It gives me a high. But after a while, I feel like returning to the organised city life—fixed work hours, clean floors, sound of vehicles, pretty shops, and people in a rush.'

Tim's phone rang and he sat down on a chair to talk. Rhea walked away to the edge of the garden thinking of her own life and of Tim's—if he really was serious about returning here. Would he do that soon? Imagine Tim not being in office. Imagine Tim sitting here, growing old on that chair surrounded by his wife and children. It was pitch dark near the hedge and she was just turning back when she spotted a tiny glint in the bushes.

'It's a glow-worm! Tim, come here, there's a glow-worm!' she called out to him. He was still talking on the phone, but looked up in her direction and immediately ended the call. He came and stood beside her.

'Oh, it was here. I saw it. It was beautiful.'

'Never seen a glow-worm before, girl?'

'Nah.'

'Go get a shawl or something and I'll take you someplace.'

'Where?'

'Go now, get your shawl. I'll go tell mom.'

The air was cold though Tim seemed unaffected in his thin tee. Rhea gathered her shawl about herself. They left the streetlights behind and came on to the dark highway. Tim took a sharp turn off the road and they were on a stony trail. As she looked over his shoulder, all she saw was darkness. The bike's headlight showed only a short stretch of the path ahead. Tim stopped at a bend. As the bike's engine and headlight died out, she heard a faint murmur of water. He held her hand and led her down a pebbled trail. The gravel crunched under their feet for some distance but where he stopped, the ground was level and grassy. He covered her eyes and led her a few steps further. Standing behind her, he lifted his hands and whispered, 'Look.'

It was a wondrous sight—like a million sparkling stars had descended before her. The glow-worms twinkled against the backdrop of a small stream flowing down the steep hillside overgrown with thick foliage. 'It's beautiful!' Caught in that mesmerising moment, Rhea felt a sudden urge to hold Tim to her, to convey to him with the tenderness that words would fall short of how her heart overflowed with love for him. 'It's beautiful!' was all she whispered.

He took her trembling hand into his and said in a voice shaking from emotion too, 'Let's go, you're cold.'

What was keeping her awake? Not guilt, nor shame. She was happy. She had experienced something she would treasure for life. But there was no denying the pain. There was a longing that was not supposed to be. She longed to let herself go. Rhea—a stream, that's what she was. That's what she wanted to be—to flow, to be wild and wanton.

Monday was Sam's birthday. He had especially invited Rhea, calling her the 'guest of honour'. Tim and his dad sat cloistered in the study with their lawyer all morning. Rhea helped around in the kitchen, walked in the garden and sunned herself. Now and then, Tim would emerge from the study and walk into the kitchen or wherever she was. He asked if she would like him to call Marina over to take her someplace, but she declined saying she was happy lazing around. She called Pankaj at eleven. He was in a meeting and told her that he'd call her back. Simi called and spoke of this and that; work and home—nothing that could hold Rhea's attention, but then she asked if Rhea was having fun.

'Yeah.'

'Make the most of it, Rhea. Let go. Don't hold back if you feel naughty,' she giggled.

'Shut up!' Rhea smiled. 'I'm having innocent fun, really. I'm very happy.'

'Good for you. But just in case…' Simi teased.

After an early lunch, Tim drove her to his friend's coffee plantation, which was closer than their own. Just a few kilometres away from town and it was another world—through a lush rainforest they came upon a verdant valley—miles and miles of gently rolling greens—the cascading coffee bushes. The view was breathtaking and the afternoon air was clean and warm. Tim held her hand as they negotiated a steep path downhill. He pointed out amidst the coffee, the cardamoms that grew in a skirt around its plant and the peppercorns that swirled around tall silver oaks.

'You too grow coffee?'

'Nah, Tea. But my dream is to grow vanilla.'

'Wow! Vanilla?'

'Yeah. We're trying it out in a small patch now. But eventually, I want to do it in a big way.'

'What does it look like?'

'It's an orchid. A vine. Grows over trees; can also on artificial structures. The vanilla comes from the pod.'

'So, is it very specialised?'

'No, not very. But just that if I start, I need to be hands on and completely involved. I don't like to not succeed. It would mean taking risks. We've done tea for so long—for generations. It's something we know well. But vanilla would be a challenge. My dad wouldn't attempt it. This is fine for him. But I have to. New things. Not there in Bangalore. But here on my land.'

Rhea nodded and felt a new respect for him.

'Tell me, do you do such impulsive things often?'

'What impulsive things?'

'Like, coming here like this…with me?'

Warmth rose to Rhea's cheeks. She smiled but kept quiet. They were heading towards a small tea stall on the roadside. 'Masala tea?'

They sat sipping the strong masala tea. 'Yes, I'm impulsive but not as many times as I would like to be. One misses out much, thinking things over. The trick is to act before discretion gets in the way.'

Tim turned to look at her and smiled. A smile that could mean a lot or nothing at all.

Rhea stood looking at herself in the mirror. She had dressed up in a peach chiffon shirt and off-white trousers for the warm evening. A string of pink pearls, matching earrings and a floral scarf completed the summery look. Tim was waiting in the car and talking to his mother standing beside it. Rhea got in quickly on the other side, not wanting aunty look too closely. Tim glanced at her once, as if to make sure she was seated and then they were off.

The car turned into a wide tree-lined lane that wound up to the Plantation Club. It was a stunningly elegant teak and stone building. The yellow lights twinkling from its spacious recesses heightened its quaint charm. A uniformed usher held the door open for her. She hadn't expected such formality and was glad she was dressed appropriately.

Sam was at the entrance. A tall, dusky girl clung to his arm. She was introduced as Sri. Pete emerged to nod a shy hello and retreated. Sara at the far end of the hall saw them and came running. She was wearing a very short black leather dress. She air kissed them both and Rhea smelled alcohol on her breath.

'You look gorgeous,' she told Rhea.

'So do you.'

There were about fifty people in the hall. At the far end was the bar and next to it a dance floor. Marina suddenly appeared with the steward carrying drinks. She was wearing a fuchsia off-shoulder, ankle-length skirt.

'Hello there!' she kissed Tim and shook Rhea's hand, 'You know something? This is the first time Timmy has brought a girl to a party. And I must warn you, at least a dozen women out there are waiting to claw you right away, hahaha! But jokes apart, tell you, everyone's going to be very, very curious about you two.' She handed Rhea a glass of wine.

Tim was engrossed in conversation with another gentleman, to whom Rhea was not introduced. Marina steered her across the hall to the bar. A large man sat smoking in a corner. 'This is my friend Simon. And this pretty lady is the one who's staying with Timmy, Rhea.' He got up to tower a couple of feet above Rhea and shook her hand firmly.

Rhea was dragged from one person to another and introduced as Timmy's friend. She looked around for Tim and spotted him talking with someone or the other. Once, she saw Sam's dusky girlfriend throw an arm over Tim's shoulder and whisper into his ear. Rhea quickly looked away.

People were slowly moving towards the crowded dance floor. Rhea stole to a couch in the corner and sat sipping the wine. As the lightness rose to her head, she smelled his aftershave. He was leaning at the back of her couch, his face very close to hers.

'Dance?'

She knew people were watching them, but the wine and the aftershave were a heady mix. He was looking into her eyes. For the first time, he was not looking away, not for a moment.

Before she knew, Tim was leading her outside. He drew her to him as they walked away on the dimly lit pathway under the ancient oaks. Once they were away from the din and the lights, he stopped and took her face in her hands. She closed her eyes.

A phone began to ring. Her cell phone. She pretended not to hear and prayed he would too. But the spell had been broken. He released her. The phone would not stop ringing. Tim had turned away and was slowly walking back—making way for her to return to her world, her husband, reason.

It was mother-in-law asking when she would return home. She was saying that Rhea must be back before her son got back. Rhea fumed. Tim was now a shadow in the distance, standing with his back to her. Mother-in-law was asking about this friend who she was staying with, 'What did you say her name was? Is she in your office? Is she married? Is her husband there too?'

Rhea answered some and ignored most. She wanted mother-in-law to feel the coldness she was feeling for her. Finally, mummyji disconnected with the final advice, 'Be back before Pankaj returns. Take care of my son.'

Tim drove back so fast, she sat clutching the seat. The house was still. Thambi answered the door and Tim disappeared up the stairs in a trice without a word to her.

It was nine when Rhea woke up. Hurriedly, she got ready and went downstairs. The house was silent as guilt. She walked out the open back door of the kitchen and found aunty in the kitchen garden overseeing a pile of dead fish being lowered into a pit near the grape vines. She smiled and said, 'You go in. Smell.'

'It's okay, Aunty I'm sorry I slept in...I'm late,' she replied, but aunty was called to another patch of the garden by a woman pulling out carrots. Rhea wandered off to the front of the house. Tim's bike stood leaning on its stand in the portico. But the white ambassador was not there.

Aunty came after her and asked if Rhea was feeling well.

'Yes, I'm fine.' She hoped aunty would tell her something about Tim because she could not make herself to ask. But aunty was busy sorting vegetables just brought in from the garden—mounds of beans, snake gourd, carrots, and tomatoes. She did not mention Timothy. When Thambi brought her tea, Rhea could hold herself no longer, 'Aunty, where are uncle and Timothy?'

'Gone.'

'Where?'

'Plantations. Timothy not tell?'

'No. When will they return? Back?'

'Night. Lunch finish, I, you go Mollyamma house. Her daughter dead. She love you.'

Aunty went back into the garden to supervise, and just as the silence began to float down on her, a vehicle pulled into the porch. Nervous, she turned to look. Marina got down from a jeep.

'Hi there, good morning!' Marina called out cheerily.

'Hi, how are you?'

'Where's everyone? I bet Tim's asleep, but where's aunty and uncle?'

'Aunty just stepped into the garden. Uncle and Tim have gone to the plantation.'

'What! He left you here and went away? So what are you doing alone in the house? Have you had breakfast? Let's go out. I'll just drop these papers with aunty.'

'Thanks, but I'm fine. You go ahead with your work.'

'What work, I'm on vacation.'

Marina stepped inside, calling out to aunty. They spoke briefly, then she turned to Rhea, 'Let's go, Rhea.'

'Really Marina, I'm fine. You don't have to go out of your way.'

'Don't be silly. I've nothing to do this morning. I'll take you for breakfast and drop you back, she's taking you someplace in the afternoon.'

Rhea went upstairs to get her bag. Marina called out to aunty, 'Aunty, powa.'

'Dosa?' She turned and asked Rhea.

'Okay.'

They stopped at a roadside eatery. 'This is the best. They make the yummiest dosas in the world. Has Tim brought you here?'

'No, we haven't had a chance. I mean, I've enjoyed the food at their place so much.'

They ordered masala dosas and coffee. Marina kept talking incessantly. 'So how long have you known Tim?'

'About a year.' Afraid that Marina might ask about their sudden disappearance from Sam's party, she elaborated, 'We're in the same team, but we sit on different floors. We don't actually meet every day, unless we're working together on a project…or if I have a problem with my PC. You know, he seems to know so much about computers, we always call him instead of the tech guys. It's so much easier. And he's so obliging.'

'Yeah, Tim's good with machines. He's always fiddling with vehicles and machines. Even as a kid he used to love ripping toys apart.'

The dosas arrived. Rhea was beginning to ask about the plantations, when a young man, presumably the owner of the restaurant, walked up to their table and started speaking to Marina in Malayalam. She spoke with him animatedly and gesturing towards Rhea said, 'Rhea, is Tim's friend from Bangalore.'

'Good morning madam, did you like the food?'

'It was wonderful, thank you.'

'Timothy always comes here. We went to the same school. He always topped the class.' After some more chit chat, he left. Rhea felt some kind of deep connection with all these people who seemed to love Tim.

'How far is the plantation from here?'

About two hours away. It's not the distance but the road is bad so it takes that long.'

'Do they have a good place to stay there?'

'Very basic. It's an office shed. But they have a private room with beds and a sort of a bath. Actually, I think it's the first time Tim would be staying there. Even when they have work for more than a day, they usually come back for the night, especially Tim. He's a stickler for clean bed and bath. Uncle is used to staying there.'

Has he gone there to avoid her? Rhea found her mood swing. She thought of how happy she'd been in the morning. It was all so complicated. She should never have got into this; she should never have come here, she despaired.

After lunch, Tim's mother and Rhea walked through the marketplace to Mollyamma's home. Mollyamma was a tall lady in her late eighties. Her scant hair was coloured coal black and plastered to her scalp in thick bands. The scaly skin from her arms drooped in big scallops, and large round gold earrings hung from elongated holes, which seemed would give way at the next shake of her head. She talked non-stop with aunty in Malayalam. She made Rhea sit close to her and patted her lovingly, calling her 'Timmy's friend' all the time. Tea was brought in on beautifully crocheted tray covers and served with thick slices of gooey, homemade ginger cake.

After tea, as the two women sat talking again, Rhea could hold herself no longer and called Tim's cell. It was not reachable. They must be on their way home already, she told herself.

Mollyamma looked at her anxious face and said, 'See house'.

It was a grand house with lime washed brick walls and high ceiling. There was dust on everything—four-poster beds, hand-carved almirahs, elegant chairs, and quaint wall clocks. One of the walls in the corridor was lined with photographs. Mollyamma, unmistakable due to her height, in her bridal gown and a gossamer veil, stood beside a stout man in a dark suit. Women in sarees with brocade borders and lace blouses, children in cotton frocks and starched shorts, Brylcreem-haired men in high-backed chairs holding pipes and walking sticks, an old Chevrolet and long-limbed dogs. Rhea wondered if Tim came here often; if he looked at these photographs and teased Mollyamma; if as a child he ran through this house and hid behind the teak cabinets and held the gooey slices of ginger cake in his grubby hands.

Rhea thought of him organising a vanilla fair. Music, games and stalls of food—all in vanilla flavour. She saw herself selling vanilla cupcakes.

When it was time to leave, Mollyamma took her into one of the rooms and opened a trunk. She took out a tattered, yellowing, sequined handbag. Inside it were several small bundles of magenta wrapping paper. She sifted through several, and then her eyes brightened as she located something.

'Timmy's friend,' she said and thrust a small magenta bundle into Rhea's palm. Inside was a pair of amethyst earrings. Rhea was taken aback. She looked at aunty.

'Take,' aunty concurred, sensing her hesitation.

Rhea remembered her father's teaching to always accept gifts graciously.

'Thank you very much, Aunty. These are lovely.' She was choked with emotion and bent forward to kiss her. Mollyamma hugged and blessed her with trembling hands.

'Timmy's friend,' she said and had tears in her eyes.

Back home, they watched TV waiting for uncle and Tim. At a little past eight, there was a phone call. Aunty talked for a while, mentioning Timothy frequently. She looked unhappy as she placed the receiver back.

'Uncle. Not coming. Work.'

'When will they come, Aunty?'

'Morning.'

They had dinner in silence and went to bed. Rhea lay in the dark room wondering where Tim was staying. She pulled the earrings out from under her pillow and looked at them in the moonlight filtering through the windows, the stones sparkled.

The day after her wedding, she was made to sit in the hall at Pankaj's parents' home in Ludhiana, dressed in all her bridal finery and gold ornaments, her head covered. The women of the neighbourhood, friends, and relatives had come for her muh deekhai. The ceremony started with Pankaj's mother lifting her veil and placing a blue, velvet covered jewellery box on Rhea's lap. 'Open beti,' someone prodded her. She opened the box. It was the most exquisite necklace and earring set Rhea had seen—a gold peacock set in emeralds and blue sapphires on a three-stringed pearl necklace and matching earrings. Even before anyone else could see it, Pankaj's elder sister, Priyanka, snatched the box from her.

'Mamma, you can't give this away.'

'I'm not giving it away, she's my bahu.'

'Give her something else, not this. This must remain in the family.'

'*She* is family.'

'How can you be so sure, mamma? What if they divorce?'

'What are you saying, Priyanka! It's inauspicious to talk like this today.'

'Mummy dear, you are so naive. I'm only saying don't be in such a hurry to give away everything to her.'

Priyanka walked away with the peacock set. Tears of humiliation stung Rhea's eyes. Mother-in-law removed her gold bangles and slipped them on Rhea's wrists.

'Don't mind, beti, Priyanka is not bad at heart. She is your nanad, always keep her happy.'

This pair of amethyst earrings meant so much to her. Gifted by Mollyamma with so much love. Rhea was no one to her, just a visitor. That Timothy had brought her there was enough for these women to love Rhea.

She got up and walked to the window. The garden below was bathed in moonlight. The coconut palms swayed gently in the breeze. She opened the window and a warm breeze swept over her. She looked at the watch—it was ten thirty. She tried Tim's cell again. No network. She took a decision.

It was Wednesday. They were to travel back that night. Rhea went downstairs early and was surprised to find uncle with his coffee, reading the newspaper.

'How are you?' he asked. And without waiting for her answer, 'Tim will come later.'

Immediately, Rhea knew she had to go ahead with her plan. 'Uncle, some urgent work has come up, and I've decided to return early. I've called for a cab; it'll be here by nine thirty.'

'But how will you go alone. Have you spoken to Timothy?'

'No Uncle, I wanted to inform him, but his phone is not reachable. It's really not a problem. I'm used to travelling alone,' she lied.

'Why didn't you tell us? There's a landline too. You made all the arrangements already? You're our responsibility. Let me call Timothy.'

'Uncle, please don't worry. I will be fine. I really must leave.'

Tim's father called his mother, and they spoke to each other in Malayalam, repeating Timothy over and over. Then his father called Tim. 'Timothy, when are you coming? Why evening?' He became a little agitated and talked in Malayalam and took Rhea's name. Finally, he gestured for her to take the phone, 'Okay, speak to her.'

She tried to sound normal. His parents were watching. 'Nah, it's fine, really. I'll go. I'm sorry I have to leave like this, but I really must.' Tim said if she could wait till the afternoon, he would accompany her. But she insisted that it was urgent.

Rhea went up to the guest room and began to gather her things. Her cell phone rang. It was an unknown landline number. Tim. She found it difficult to contain all the emotions now that they had the privacy. She wanted to ask him why he'd left without telling her and why he hadn't called. Tears were threatening to rise in her voice, but she managed to sound composed.

'As long as you are in Kerala, you're my responsibility. Wait for me, I'm coming. I'll take you home. We'll reach by late night.'

The tenderness in those words made her want to hurt him more. 'I am no one's responsibility. I'm quite capable of taking care of myself. Bye, Tim and thanks for everything.'

'Damn.'

She looked down wistfully at the kitchen garden and at the tea estates far away. She wanted to capture everything in her memory. Tim's mother embraced her and handed her a bag with food for the journey. She also handed her another parcel—a Kerala saree, white and gold. Rhea felt tears clouding her vision. She thanked Tim's parents and invited them to her home in Bangalore.

As the taxi drove past the green lawn and the palm-lined driveway, Rhea strained herself to catch a last glimpse of everything.

Late afternoon, her phone rang. It was Tim.

'Where have you reached?'

'We're two hours away, I guess.'

There was silence.

'Are you back home?' She asked.

'Yes, I missed you by about twenty minutes.'

There was another pause.

'How are you?' he asked.

Tears welled up and a sense of deep distress weighed her voice down, 'Okay.' After a pause to collect herself, she said, 'I had such a wonderful time with you all. Thank you, Tim, for everything.'

'Rhea, I'm really sorry.'

She kept quiet.

'Take care, Rhea. Call me the moment you reach home.'

'I will.'

Pankaj opened the door and turning away mumbled something like a response to her hi. She lugged her bag into the bedroom and proceeded to unpack. He sat watching soccer in the living room. After a shower when she stepped into the bedroom, Pankaj was already fast asleep. Angry as she felt, she tried not to make noise. In the kitchen, she found an unopened box of pizza presumably left there for her. There was another empty box and two empty cans of beer on the counter and crumbs everywhere. She put the pizza into the microwave to heat and started cleaning up. It was almost eleven when she got to bed but lay awake.

Pankaj woke her up at eight thirty the next morning to say he was leaving for work. She pulled the covers over her head. At ten thirty, she finally got out of bed, made herself some coffee and sat watching TV.

At twelve when the house help came and began cleaning, Rhea took a quick shower and went out to the supermarket.

When Pankaj returned in the evening, the house was gleaming in the beautiful light of the crystal chandelier and the candles she'd set on the tables. She'd put fresh tuberoses in the foyer and the bedroom. The dining table was set in his favourite royal blue colour.

Pankaj chose to remain gruff and walked into the bedroom leaving his shoes and bag in the hall. She picked after him without a word and got him a glass of water, which he took from her without meeting her gaze. While he was in the shower, she looked at herself in the mirror again and dabbed some more of the green apple fragrance he loved.

Pankaj deposited himself on the sofa before the TV. Rhea poured wine in two glasses and placing it on the table before them, came to sit next to him. Pankaj did not touch the wine but got himself a can of beer from the fridge. He sat drinking without once looking at her.

Rhea moved closer to him and slid her arm through his. Her green-apple-smelling hair, still moist from the wash, fell on his shoulder. He did not seem to mind but remained stiff, eyes fixed on soccer. After another beer, she felt his body relax. He sank deeper into the couch and did not flinch when she touched his mouth. He was yielding. She closed her eyes and waited. Tim carried her inside to their bed. All night she saw glow-worms.

You will never get to edit another book of mine. T texted.

Why?

Because there won't be another.

Offo!

Being a strong woman is a bane, really. Once you are tagged as one, everyone expects you to deal with everything on your own, so much so that the strong woman becomes someone everyone can easily ignore, overlook, as though she doesn't exist. Till they need her. Did I do that to her? Placed her on a pedestal from where she could not come down when her back hurt from the strain of the pretence?

I asked myself if I had been unnecessarily pushy. Why would I push her? It was difficult to admit it to myself, but that's the truth—she was my golden goose. One builds an editing career over long, slow years but once you get tagged as a popular writer's editor, there is much that comes with it apart from the regular work and money. Recognition is an addictive soul food.

But I swear, I didn't do it for myself, I genuinely liked her and her writing.

Some reactions in this collection are so alien to who T is. But then, 'Distance,' she would say, 'We need distance from our characters and plots—otherwise, we will only speak our own minds every time they open their mouths.'

Mary

What was in there? Very afraid of what she might find, she looked into the pot of bubbling water on the stove to which she'd just added a spoonful of tea leaves. Two eyes stared back at her. His piercing red eyes, small, and vicious. The harder she looked the more his eyes bored into her. She forgot to turn the gas off, and the one cup water receded leaving chai rings and tea leaves stuck to the sides.

Whatever she did to push his face away, didn't work. Sometimes he was behind the pile of clothes in the wardrobe. She never reached out there to look for something unless someone else was in the room, and all the lights were switched on. The wardrobe remained shut tight, at all other times.

Like nausea, fear rose, without forewarning. How hard she tried to not remember. She would suddenly begin to sing along with a song on the radio, or clean a window till it shone like there was no glass. But just as she would begin to relax, he would come back—at the bookshop, restaurant, office, grocery, anywhere she went he followed her.

Back home, he was always there, following her as she went about her life. Tending to her lilies, she knew he would be standing there, right behind her, to stare into her terrified eyes if she were to turn around. Folding the laundry, she felt if she wasn't quick enough, he would hand her the next piece of clothing as her hand reached towards the pile. He followed her wherever she went in his dirty kurta pyjama, his bloodshot eyes, and his missing left foot.

Suddenly, Mary appeared before her. She was washing clothes in the open field. Squatting over the stone slabs with the water gushing below her, washing fervently as always. Mary looked up as Swati's feet reached the bundle of soapy, well-beaten clothes. Their eyes met.

'Mary, when did you come back?'

Her eyes rounds of terror, Mary only muttered, 'He's alive.'

'Oh!' Swati gasped.

'They cut off his left foot. But he is alive.'

Swati collected herself and, bending down to touch Mary's

shoulder to reassure, whispered, 'Good, no one needs to know anything about it, okay?' But the whites of Mary's eyes were already growing larger.

She looked towards a footfall behind Swati. Swati heard it too and knew he was upon them. Too terrified to turn and look, she shot past Mary and ran towards the house as fast as she could. She had to make sure.

The rickety back door was ajar. She closed it shut behind her and fixed the chain latch firmly. The shovel was lying in a heap of manure where the mali had left it near the jumbled pile of tools. She picked it and ran to the far end of the courtyard. Frantically, she began digging the mud. It was still soft.

She dug and dug, but nothing—no limbs, no flesh, no bone—nothing. Only soft mud. He was gone. He was alive. Was it more terrifying to have him alive than dead? At least now no one needed to know what she...they did.

Mary had appeared at her doorstep one foggy winter morning. Swati was getting late for office and was impatient with her mumbling and indirect answers. The current maid, Durga was leaving and had sent this woman as her replacement.

Swati's anger at Durga found an outlet in her first interaction with Mary. But the prospect of living another day without help seemed daunting, so she decided to ask Mary to come back in the evening.

That foggy morning as she stood looking down from the main door, coffee in hand, at this dark bony woman, fidgeting with her dupatta ends, her feet resting on two different doorsteps, she had no forewarning of how deeply their lives were going to get entwined and how this one decision to employ her would change her own life forever.

For the next couple of years there was no cause for worry. Within a month, Mary became a part of the family. Cheerful and warm, she kept the children happy. Some evenings when Swati returned from work, she could hear their laughter emerging from the lit up windows. Mary seemed much attached to the kids. She worried if they developed the slightest sign of cold or fever. She stayed back if Swati was late at work.

Mary also looked after the house well. In the beginning, Swati on returning from work would take off her shoes and slip her bare feet behind furniture and in the corners to check for dust. All maids, left to themselves, resorted to such tricks—leave some corners and under-the-tables upswept, some side-tables undusted, some plants unwatered. But she found no fault with Mary.

Every morning, Mary appeared at eight sharp. While Swati finished her breakfast, Mary busied herself with cleaning the entrance and decorating it with a rangoli—a fresh design every day. Patiently, she pinched out the powder into white dots and then joined them with delicate twirls till an intricate pattern emerged. Neat outlines. Perfect symmetry.

Some days it would be drastically different. Mary would sprinkle bright pink powder into large flower petals. The flowers seemed angry when the yellows, the greens, and the purples were added. Then, the calm white welcome to the house turned into an angry *stay away*! Swati let Mary be. She just leapt over the flowers on her way out hoping they would not pulsate so much when she returned in the evening.

The whole day, Mary cleaned and washed and dusted the house. At four in the afternoon, she went to pick the kids from their bus stop. It was quite a walk from home and on their way back, the kids played pranks and teased her. They would run ahead of her and she would try to catch up calling after them, anxious for their safety. In the evening, she would complain to Swati that the children never listen to her. Just as Swati would begin to scold them, Mary would smile and muffle her giggles in her dupatta.

Swati soon grew quite fond of Mary. She went out of her way to help her. She gave her food and clothes generously. Any article, which lay unused in the house would be offered to Mary if she had need for it—she always did. Whenever Swati bought mithai, some was set aside for Mary's family. Whenever she got chocolates for her children, she got some for Mary's too.

If Mary was not well, she was asked to take rest and not do the housework. On Christmas and on both kids' birthdays, Swati bought Mary a new saree. A relative had once given Swati a green bedspread with bright pink flowers painted over it. When on Christmas, Swati handed it to Mary, Mary seemed thrilled. It was shown around to Mary's family, relatives, and visitors with pride and won a lot of praise from them for Swati.

Mary lived next door to her aged parents with her three sons and husband, a house painter, who spent much of his life doing nothing, staying home drunk. Her old father tended to plants in a few apartments. Some days, Mary's face would be sullen in the morning. When asked she'd quietly draw Swati into the corner of the kitchen and tell her how her drunk husband had fought and taken away her all her money, her savings. Several times Swati asked Mary to bring him home so Swati could talk and drive some sense into him. But he never came.

Then one day, Mary was ill and her husband came to inform that she wouldn't come for a few days. That was the first time Swati saw him. Her first reaction was—he cannot be Mary's husband! His bloodshot eyes sent a chill inside her. He did not look up much while speaking to her, but when he did, his piercing eyes held her with an unknown dread. Long after he left, a compelling sense of disquiet stayed with Swati. Eventually, she managed to convince herself that since she had nothing to do with him, she needn't worry.

Some days later, when Mary came back, she suggested they call her father to re-pot the plants. Swati agreed instantly but later worried that her husband might also come along. She did not have the courage to ask Mary or tell her to not get him. How could she do that? He was Mary's husband. Mary, who poured her heart into the care of her house and her children. How could Swati ask her that? Also, she had no basis for her fear.

One Sunday, she saw him following the old man on a bicycle on which they carried a sack, full of soil and compost. The plants were pulled out of the pots, their soil shaken off, the pots emptied and then filled with a fresh mix of soil and compost and the plants potted again. The old man worked hard, the son-in-law lingered till the job was done—doing little and not speaking at all. Swati handed the money to Mary's father and against all warnings of her senses, shot a glance at his workmate. His face was expressionless as he looked back straight into Swati's eyes. Fear anchored itself in Swati's heart.

Swati began to notice that Mary's husband was always around the apartment gate when she returned late from work. Casually, she mentioned it to Mary who said he comes to take her home when it gets late.

One day, Mary asked for leave. Her husband had injured his foot and she had to go to the hospital with him. When Swati told her that she had an important meeting that day and could not skip office, Mary did not insist. Calmly, she changed the arrangement. Her mother went with her husband. That evening, he hit her.

Four days later, Mary again said she wanted to go to the hospital because due to the pain in his foot, her husband was unable to go to work and earn. She took the morning off.

Two days later, Radha casually mentioned during dinner that Mary's husband had come to the bus stop with Mary to pick them. The spoon slipped from Swati's hand back into the bowl of dal, splattering some on the tablecloth. What was he doing around her children? She wanted the details. Radha told her that his foot was swollen and he could not walk properly. He did not have slippers too, Radha seemed sorry for him. Did he say anything to them? Did he walk with them? Did he look at them? Swati's stomach felt queasy.

Next morning, she lingered over small talk with Mary and asked about her husband. The trouble with the foot refuses to go, she learnt. Is he going to work? No. Was he at the bus stop with her? Yes, he was returning after seeing another new doctor.

Her husband had apparently stepped on something sharp, probably a nail, while painting. Swati wondered if something was still there—logged into his flesh. She took out a pair of unused slippers and giving them to Mary for him, and asked her to take him to a good doctor at the earliest. But the thought of him wearing the slippers she was holding in her hands made her drop them on the floor.

Days, weeks, went by. They changed doctors and they changed medicines, but Mary's husband continued to suffer. One doctor advised an incision while another prescribed ointment. The left foot did not heal. He suffered terrible pain, according to Mary. Mary started losing her verve. Her face was permanently lined with worry. Swati often told her that the problem may be more serious than they thought, and proper treatment was required. One day, when Swati was particularly irritated, she looked at Mary's sullen face and shouted without thinking, 'You will realise your stupidity when they chop his leg off!'

Then on, Mary became quieter. She did not mention her husband's suffering. It suited Swati but she felt helpless when she asked, and in response Mary held out an imaginary melon to show how his foot had swollen.

After several months, when he was no better, he was finally admitted to the hospital for surgery. The afternoon he was to be operated upon, Swati went to the hospital after work. There was no sign of them. Swati realised that she did not know his name, but by describing his condition she was able to get information about him. They had discharged him. Discharged already?

'Sister!' She followed a nurse, 'Sister, this man with the injured foot who was to be operated?'

'They went 'ome.'

'The operation was okay?'

'No operation, ma. They took him inside, but when the surgeon saw his condition, he said to take him to a big hospital. We can't handle such serious cases here, ma. He will have to go to a big hospital only.'

'Sister, please tell me what is wrong with his foot.'

'Gangrene.'

A very nervous Swati knocked on Mary's door. Mary opened the door and Swati could hear his groans. He had been administered painkillers, but wracked with pain, he was wailing. Swati sat in silence with Mary outside her tin-roofed home. There were no words to exchange. Mary described the morning ordeal briefly and then fell silent. When she got up to leave, Swati tried again to convince her to go to a good doctor. All night, Swati heard his piercing wails.

All the hospitals they visited recommended amputation. The family did not see it as a possibility. They refused. The man was dying from the pain. He would not let Mary out of his sight.

When in pain, he would pull her hair and hit her in his helplessness. Mary would try to comfort him as best as she could and then unable to bear his beatings would run outside and cry. When she thought about his foot, Swati had visions of a lab full of jars, containing limbs and body parts in formaldehyde as Mohan in her office had once described. Among those, a foot—a putrid left foot, sitting on the top shelf.

Then, one day, in a fit of rage and helplessness when he hit her, Mary began to hit him back. Then, all of a sudden, they were in Swati's backyard, fighting for their lives. Mary's desperate cries for help, drew Swati outside. And Swati, in a final attempt to end his tyranny over Mary, hit him as hard as she could. They, Mary and she, stabbed him with kitchen knives. He fell down writhing in pain, bleeding. He was dead for them. They covered him up in the loose soil in the backyard. Mary went off to her village with her sons.

Now she was back. So was he. His left pyjama-leg dangling as he hobbled on a pair of crutches. He was coming after Swati. He was there, lingering near the apartment gate when she returned from work. He was there, hiding behind the postman when she answered the door. He was there, in her room when she came out of the bathroom in her bathrobe.

Gone Girl. *She had thrown the book on my coffee table and said, 'Debika, I hated it.'*

'Really? I found it unputdownable.'

'But for the revenge, the lust, and the cheating, there is nothing. Makes you wary of people, doesn't it? There is no redeeming human emotion there.'

I thought about it later and quite agreed. I gave the book away to the circulating library in our complex. And now T is writing about revenge, lust, and cheating.

But I forsook T. 'Forsook' is the kind of word, she would have cringed at—'Debika, did they use it a lot in your time? 15th century, was it?' I would mock-hit her on her head with a book within my reach.

No point denying it. She was everything I was not—fun, carefree, successful. I envied her; her easy charm.

Games

Pia sat studying the dalmoth in the bowl. Staying focussed, she took out the deep-fried, masala speckled cashew nuts first. Having devoured those, she rummaged for the melon seeds, which stuck to her moist fingertips and she just licked them off. She tossed the bowl and some more ivory-smooth seeds surfaced. Finally, the bowl had only the shiny black, deep fried, masoor dal and the minute nylon sev.

Choosing between *two* was wrong. She began to spoon the mixture into her mouth.

Back when she was a little pig-tailed girl of seven, she was waiting at the bus stop with her mother when another woman came with twin girls her age. The woman scooped out a handful of colourful sweet saunf from a packet into the palms of the girls to keep them occupied while they waited for their bus. Had it been one girl, Pia was sure, the woman would have noticed her and offered her some too. But, between the two of them, the girls did not need any other.

The twins devised a game, Pia watched them play. One girl called out a colour—pink—and both started picking and popping all the pinks into their mouths. Pinks over, the other chose a colour. Green, purple, orange, white—saunf by saunf, colour by colour, they devoured the entire handful. Pia looked on with rapt interest, the taste of the sugar-coated fennel seed bursting in her mouth. But they took no notice of her. They had each other.

The dalmoth began to rise inside her. She opened the fridge and took a swig of iced water straight from the bottle. It seemed to douse the fires in her stomach. But the concoction began to rise again. She rushed into the bathroom and threw up. Lying on bed to let the sickness subside, she knew she would soon be looking for something to eat again. But first, she must clean.

She filled a bucket of water and emptied it over the floor of her studio apartment. She emptied another. And more till it reached every nook and it looked as though her fourteenth-floor home was flooding. She watched it lick her feet and the legs of the all-purpose table and two chairs and the single bed. Leaving a wet water line on everything, it began trickling away into the bathroom.

Daintily, like salt over an enormous omelette, Pia sprinkled detergent powder on the wet floor. White foam rose as the wiper grazed the floor tiles. Back and forth she worked, cleaning each tile, each row—one, two...twelve tiles; then one, two, twelve. She bent down to reach under the bed and some dirt, stuck unseen, came floating out magically. Fluff and hair, a yellow button, a black hair pin, and the back of an earring. She scrubbed a few tough stains and watched the soft ones melt. She brought in more water to wash off the suds.

The floor became clean. She had dusted every surface of the house a little while earlier, wearing cotton gloves that were now being run in the washing machine—two white gloves in one wash cycle. There was not a speck of dust or fingerprint anywhere, not a crease on the bed.

She got into the shower, flossed, and soaked her feet in a tub. She stood under the almost scalding water, scrubbed herself, and shampooed her hair twice. Then patting herself dry and tying her hair in the towel, she sat on the rim of the tub and rubbed in the moisturiser over her warm, moist skin.

She stood up and inspected her body—not a single blemish, except one—the abrasion on the right thigh, which was healing. She covered it up by bringing her thighs close together and stood looking at herself in the fogged out bathroom mirror.

The house smelt clean. The floor was dry and cool. Her arms and legs ached. She was tired. It had been a long day at work. But *she* still kept coming back—that Richa Lall. How frail she had looked on the hospital bed this morning—tubes in and out of her body, equipment beeping behind her. A shadow of the Richa Lall she had watched. Daily.

The first time she noticed Richa Lall was when she saw her in her brand new, red car with Pawan. Pia had looked away, but when Pawan called later to say that 'Richa' was treating him to lunch, to celebrate her new car, she had instinctively sensed the beginning of an end. She had never spoken with Richa Lall till then. After that, there was no reason.

Richa Lall sat at the far end from her workstation and it was easy to look in her direction in a general, casual sort of way. Pia got a good look at her each day—what she wore, how she walked, talked, and when she could, Pia also looked at her lunch tray. It didn't help that Richa Lall was abundantly attractive, self-assured, and stylish. Pia hoped for a day when Richa Lall's kurta would not be properly ironed or the heel of her four-inch stilettos would come off, bang in the middle of her hoity-toity walk, or perhaps, a hint of a paunch would show beneath her tight shirt. Wishful thinking. Richa Lall was perfection personified.

On days she spotted Pawan having coffee with Richa Lall in the cafeteria or the two of them leaving together in the evening, she walked to the sweet shop next to the office and bought samosas and mithai to come back to her empty flat and eat till she was sick.

Soon Pawan drifted away from her in a very definite way that did not require any talk, call, email, anything.

At an office event, when she was thrown into a team of three, it was her luck that the other two were Richa Lall and Pawan. While she jotted down the ideas for the team challenge with a shaking hand, she glanced at them—their heads very close together and fingers interlinked under the table—whispering, giggling, and looking deep into each other's eyes. Pia did not exist for them. They had no need of her. They had each other.

Pia tore up a square piece of paper from a notebook and curling it into a cone, filled it with channa-chur. Squeezing a lemon over it, she sat in the balcony eating from the cone. She was back in school with a canteen-bought paper cone of channa-chur. School days. No boys. No choosing. No losing.

But as she sat in the unlit corner of the balcony, Richa Lall came back to her. It was 2.30 am.

That morning when she had reached her office, there was a crowd at the reception. Richa Lall was in the hospital. Critical. Attempted suicide.

What is 'attempted' suicide? An empty threat. If you want to die then make sure you do. Why linger? Why half die?

A group was going to see Richa Lall at the hospital. Pia went along. She had to know.

Everyone stood solemnly around Richa Lall's hospital bed. Some said nice things in sympathy-laden, unclear voices. Someone tried to joke. Someone else tried to hold her hand. Richa Lall didn't look up to meet anyone's eye.

They started to file out of the room. As the crowd around her seemed to dissolve, Pia found herself unable to move and was suddenly alone in the room with Richa Lall. She moved a little closer to the bed. When Richa Lall did not look up, she turned to leave. And just then, a hand grabbed hers.

Panicked, Pia looked towards the door, hoping someone had lingered. No one. She was alone in the room with Richa Lall, who had tried to kill herself and had not died.

Then, she heard a rasping voice, of the one who had nearly died the night before, speak to her.

'This is between us. He cheated on me. I can neither live with him nor without. I'm going to kill myself.' Richa Lall looked straight into the startled eyes of Pia.

No one was there to witness this, to recall, recount, tell, testify. Pia pulled her hand out of Richa Lall's cold clench and turned to leave. At the door, she heard, clear and firm, 'It'll be tonight and this time there will be no mistake.'

Pia stopped at the door, turned back and smiled at Richa Lall. She hadn't heard a thing. Richa Lall was sick; in the hospital for attempted suicide. She could be hallucinating.

She crushed the empty paper cone in her hand and rushed to the bathroom.

Maybe my lecturing drove her away. Maybe I wasn't really listening to her. Just always ready with advice, dismissing her anxiety.

Nothing 'fighty' ever happened between the two of us. In fact, when we met in October, at a play, she hugged me for a full two minutes as we stood surrounded by people in the lobby. She was looking very cheerful and chic.

She introduced me to her husband's cousin, Sue who was with her. She said Sue was a very promising writer, and that I must take her under my wing. When I asked Sue if she had something ready, T replied that she'd soon be ready with a book. That was T. Not an iota of envy.

Perhaps, the publisher wanted another editor. Am I too set in my ways?

Yesterday, AA publishers asked me to be the jury for their annual short story competition. They sent me a cheque and the shortlisted stories that I have to rate.

I'm reading and quite enjoying the new voices, fresh perspectives and the sparkling youthfulness. They sound like young writers to me—the names and other details are not disclosed.

The Kirtan Group

There can be no middle path. You can either be with them or be completely alienated. If you choose the first, you ought to be prepared to answer all their questions—ranging from how many children to whether the marriage is love or arranged—all at the very first meeting even if it is on the staircase as you are huffing and puffing your way up your second-floor flat, hauling a ten-kg grocery bag. If you choose not to, you'd be gossiped about endlessly.

This, Aprajita learned early about Delhi housing societies. The grapevine was like a fresh stream charting its course. One had no control; no one had.

The wellspring of gossip for the grapevine was beyond doubt the kirtan group that met on Tuesdays. A simple line such as, 'I saw someone move into 301' had to be dropped to have all the details about the new neighbour—furnished by Mrs Mehra, Mrs Krishnan, Mrs Gupta, Mrs Malhotra, Mrs Khanna, Mrs Puri, and Mrs Arora.

Soon after this, the new neighbour would be met with knowing smiles from everyone, a question, or a comment meant to convey that they knew them, rather, about them, especially, if they had a tag attached—such as an inter-caste marriage, a divorce, an adopted child—or even something or someone they may be associated with—a company that went bankrupt, an aunt who committed suicide, or a cousin who was a model.

Visits would follow—from Mrs Mehra, who'd walk straight into the bedroom, carrying a katori, and ask for jaaman only after she was comfortably seated with both her saree-draped legs up on the bed, her pallu released from the shoulder to lie on her lap; to Rita Kumar, who'd come to ask for the maid only to add if she could leave her three-year-old for an hour as she had a beauty parlour appointment.

Aprajita moved into a top-floor flat of one such housing society with her two children—14-year-old Kavya and four-year-old Krishn.

'Bada gap', the women whispered.

'Husband?' Mehra Aunty asked.

'Oh, he is in foreign,' Arora Aunty replied even as her bahu almost chided her, 'New Zealand, Mummyji!'

So Aprajita, whose husband worked with the goras and

earned in dollars, was inducted into the kirtan group. Aprajita hastened into becoming one of them, giving them no time to form an opinion about her.

As soon as she settled into her new flat, she let her wet towel fall into the balcony below. Entering Mrs Nanda's ghee-smelling home, seeing her roasting besan for laddus, she took the jhaara from her and nudged her gently aside, 'Hato Auntiji, let me do it, you must be tired.' She knocked at Mrs Narayan's house at three in the afternoon to say, 'Auntyji, Krishn's nose is bleeding, please come and see.' On bumping into Mrs Malhotra on the stairs, she chirped, 'Auntyji, you will live a hundred years! I was just thinking of you. You know, we have this puja on the fifteenth day of sawan; what is it called? My mother used to prepare malpuas. I want to do it. Children should know our traditions, na.'

The older ladies were won over thus. For the younger ones, she had a different strategy. 'Please Rekha, can you help me drape the saree? You wear it like a model,' and 'Pooja, how do you manage the home and your full-time job so well? I'm envious.'

Soon everyone knew what she cooked, which agarbatti she used, how much the kids scored. If she was seen taking the car out at a particular time of the day, the ladies knew it was time for her to pick Krishn from the drawing classes.

She would rush into Mathur Aunty's lawn on the ground floor and call out to let her know that she was spreading her washing on Mathur Aunty's clothesline as she did not get enough sun in her own balcony.

There was no need to ask. This was also at the risk of Mathur Aunty touching the clothes to gauge their wetness and confiding to the others, who sat there shelling peas in the sun, after Aprajita had left, 'Washed by hand, not in machine.'

'No, no, she has a washing machine. I have seen it,' someone would supply, adding, 'it's light green.'

Each day, she discussed with the ladies whatever they thought pressing—the chowkidar's affair with the dhooban, pickling of jackfruit, current width of salwar-poncha, or if indeed Mrs Sahni's new daughter-in-law's nose was not as theekhi as Arora Aunty's daughter-in-law's.

Since she lived alone, it was assumed that nothing was too pressing in Aprajita's life. In the evening when the ladies dispersed abruptly in bunches as the street lights came on, Aprajita would be detained till the last of them found something important to do.

Very often, Aprajita could be heard screaming at Krishn—her enraged voice piercing their thin common walls and reaching the neighbours through bathroom ducts and balconies. The old ladies, warming their knobby knees in the winter sun, would then tut-tut and say to each other how difficult it was to bring up a son in the absence of a father. Everyone sympathised with Aprajita for managing her household and kids alone.

It rained on Karva Chauth so the ladies gathered in Aprajita's flat for the evening puja. Aprajita looked stunning in a black silk saree with a wide gold border, her hair tied up in a knot, kajal outlining her not-so-prominent eyes, and a large gold pendant in braided black silk around her neck.

But black? On an auspicious occasion like this, when women were in reds, pinks, and magentas? But Aprajita was now so much a part of their group that no one seemed to mind. If they did, they did not speak, afraid of not finding consensus or worse, being thought a prude, as had happened with Mrs Bhalla.

Mrs Bhalla had commented one day that Mrs. Malhotra's daughter-in-law was seen in a nighty on the balcony. Her precise words were, 'Imagine walking in front of your father-in-law in a thin nighty!'

Mrs Naidu, whose married daughter wore trousers to office, was quick to block the coming barrage of disapproval by saying, 'Zamana badal raha hai, it's better to change our own outlook.' To Mrs Bhalla's surprise, all the women had nodded in agreement.

But back to Karva Chauth, the women sat in a circle holding their puja thalis decorated with glowing ghee diyas, water in tumblers, mithai, and mattis. Mrs. Malhotra narrated the story of Santo, whose slip-up during the Karva Chauth fast had caused many afflictions, including her husband's body being riddled by countless needles. This bit never failed to create an upsurge of awe among the ladies. They became very solemn. Mrs Malhotra continued the story. Santo was rewarded for her goodness and punished for her mistakes.

As she stopped after each episode, the women sang the chorus and passed their thalis around. This was invariably interrupted by the re-lighting of diyas, arranging of pallus that kept slipping off their heads, sending Pinkus to fetch matches, and instructions to Bunties to sit quietly. At one point, it was interrupted by Aprajita when she called out to Kavya to take photographs.

Kavya came out of her room and began clicking photos with her phone. Aprajita directed her all the time, and when Kavya seemed done, she instructed her to keep the phone carefully in the bedroom.

'These imported phones,' she said, 'are so nazuk, we have to be very careful. You know na, what happened last time?'

The explanation of the 'last time' was presumably furnished for those who hadn't heard it before. No one had. It so happened, she explained, that her husband did not get enough leave to come home every year, 'So, I told him, "Don't worry, I'll come halfway," and leaving the children with my parents, I went to see him in Singapore. We took soooo many photographs together but on the way back, I touched some button and everything was wiped out!'

But for all her affability, Aprajita's outbursts were growing. One day, when one of the kids asked Krishn if his papa had another mummy in foreign like his own mausaji, and all the kids began to laugh, Krishn landed a slick punch in the boy's face. Hearing him bawl, all mothers congregated. In a fit of rage, Aprajita started hitting Krishn.

The ladies pulled him away and tried to calm Aprajita. But when some mothers feigning anger at their own kids went overboard and got completely taken in by the general wave of sympathy for Krishn, Aprajita changed her stance abruptly. She began screaming at the other children, accusing them of bullying Krishn. The other mothers were taken aback.

The women deliberated and discussed with each other at dining tables with their husbands and during TV soap breaks with mothers-in-law. Finally, they came to the conclusion that Aprajita was after all not as agreeable as they had first thought her to be. The practical ones concluded that she was going through 'those days'; the more considerate ones agreed that loneliness was after all getting the better of her.

A couple of days after the children's fight, the old dadu, in the block opposite Aprajita's, passed away. The food on the kriya day was being prepared at Mrs Sharma's house.

Mrs Sharma had already prepared aloo-tamater, sweet and sour kaddu, boondi raita, and peas pulao. Just as the people began to arrive, turning the solemn atmosphere lighter by jokes that would not have otherwise been funny, a flurry of ladies pushed their way into Mrs Sharma's tiny kitchen to help make the pooris—a continuous supply of which would be needed for the next couple of hours.

Some of the women had come with their own rolling pins, for their hands were set on those. Some of them sat on the floor rolling out the dough, and some took position before the woks brimming with oil on the gas stove, ready for frying. In walked Aprajita and deftly took charge of the frying, gently pushing away Mrs Narayan, who was at the stove.

Now, the flat disks of dough entering the hot oil in one wok came out puffed as balls, but those out of Aprajita's remained tight and flat.

'She's making papads,' the women spoke in muffled voices.

Aprajita expertly splashed oil on the pooris, but to no avail—the pooris in her wok remained downright flat. After dishing out about ten such, Aprajita complained that the wok in which she was frying was not okay.

'The one I have is perfect—light and deep. Pooris come out so well and so fast.'

Mrs Sharma was rightly miffed, 'I always fry in this one. I've never had problems.'

The rest of the women nodded their heads and clicked their tongues in agreement, both when Aparajita spoke as well as Mrs Sharma did. It was difficult to say who they supported, which side they were on.

Eventually, Aprajita's complaints grew so irksome that the entire concern of feeding people, patiently waiting for the next thaliful of pooris, was obscured by the suitability of the karahi. Irritated at the sight of huge piles of flat pooris and worried at the prospect of more such, Rita spoke, 'Why don't you get your karahi, Bhabhiji? We can do it so much faster then.'

Mrs Sharma's maid was hurriedly dispatched to get it. The

wok, when fetched from Aprajita's home, was discovered to be much the same. Mrs Sharma felt avenged. She squared her shoulders and tucked the end of her saree into her waist, ready for the challenge. The other women hid their mocking smiles in their saree pallus, as Aprajita continued to dish out flat pooris but without any complaints now.

When Aprajita did not turn up for the kirtan on Tuesday, the general presumption was that it was due to her 'monthly,' but her recent falling out of favour with the ladies had instigated some amount of antagonism in everyone's heart. The discussions about her that had taken place in each home needed to be aired, but not before the women were sure that they were all united in their opinion of her. This had to be prodded deftly. So the sarcasm in the simple, 'Today Aprajita didn't come?' was duly acknowledged and moved to, 'Of what use is money if you can't live with your family?' and very quickly to the next level, 'Wonder if there *is* a husband.'

When they realised that no one had actually seen her husband or a photo of him, the ladies became very excited. Each one wanted to prove that she had found out long ago, and before anyone else, that something was amiss; that they always suspected she was not as sweet and *gen-noo-aine* as she looked.

As the discussion progressed, their suspicion gained more ground. They were now certain that a husband did not exist. He had not visited in two years, and Aprajita had never talked of him; never said, 'My husband does not like bhindi.' How cleverly she had fooled them!

What they had to find out now was whether she was divorced or if he had left her. Maybe, she wasn't married at all? At this suggestion, hands flew to cover mouths, open with shock and concern of not having control over the type of people moving into the society, and the bad influence they would be on the children, grew loud.

What was Aprajita's big secret? A plan was carefully chalked out to find this out. Mrs Malhotra was to lead the investigation. She would visit Aprajita to enquire why she had not come for the kirtan. She would casually ask to see Aprajita's wedding album. If Aprajita made an excuse, she would ask where her in-laws lived. Whichever town she named, Mrs Malhotra would mention that her son was going there and ask for her in-laws' address or phone number, so he could pay his regards. Once they had a phone number or address, they could always find out if she was lying. And if Aprajita evaded this, their fears would be considered well founded.

A Plan-B was also chalked out, in case Mrs Malhotra's mission failed. Mrs Malhotra was miffed at such a suggestion but was quickly mollified. Mrs Nanda said that she could win Aprajita's confidence by telling her about her own imaginary niece whose husband had left her. Listening to the heart-wrenching tale, everyone agreed that Mrs Nanda was sufficiently skilled at spinning tales and that Aprajita would certainly give away something.

The gaggle of women returned to their homes—to cook, to send children to tuitions, to watch family sagas on TV. Work seemed light that evening, the daily drudgery had disappeared. Those who did not know the reason would have wondered why the ladies of the kirtan group appeared so amiable. Every once in a while, they could be seen outside—in the balcony or the corridor, either at the pretext of straightening out the clothes, long dry on the clothesline, or picking rice or just stretching a hand out to check if it was beginning to rain. They could be seen stealing furtive glances towards Aprajita's flat, and at times exchanging knowing smiles with each other.

At 9 pm, Mrs. Nanda called up to tell Mrs Krishnan that Mrs Malhotra had called her to say that Aprajita was not home. So Mrs Nanda was to carry out her plan the next morning. The ladies were a little disappointed. The wait had been stretched.

The next morning, at ten, Rani was spreading out her washing in her front yard when Mrs Sharma passed by and they began talking. When Mrs Sharma drew close to her and in a hushed tone, said, 'Let's see what happens today!' both smiled.

This was observed by Aarti in the balcony upstairs, who called out, 'Hello ji! Has the sabziwalli come?' And not waiting for their answer, 'Achcha, never mind, I'll only come down.'

Mrs Agarwal on her way back from the dentist, holding her palm over her swollen jaw, and spitting out blood, sat down on a step near Rani's front yard, as if to rest. Seeing them, Mrs Malhotra, who had ventured into her balcony, also came down.

All of them talked in hushed tones. The excitement was palpable. They were just waiting for Mrs Nanda to come out.

'Rani, call her up once, na. What if she forgets?' someone said.

'Arre, how can that be?' They laughed in collective glee.

A taxi, balancing several bulky suitcases tied to its roof with a yellow nylon rope, came to a halt at the main gate just then. The security guard peered inside and opened the gates wide. All eyes turned automatically towards it as mouths, finding no ears, stopped mid sentence.

The taxi came to a stop inside the gate in full view of the watching women. The front door opened, and a ruddy foreigner, his hair and eyes light, stepped out. Krishn, who sat with him, jumped out and seeing the ladies shouted excitedly, 'Dekho, my papa has come!'

'It has dried up,' she announced, as she entered my home and sunk into the nearest chair, 'shrivelled and fallen.'

'What has?' I kept the book I was reading, down.

'Imagination, my dear Debika. My imagination!'

I lost it that day. I lost it because I felt helpless. I yelled back, 'Stop playing victim! And you know what? Maybe it is *over, maybe it* has *run dry. There are people who write only one book or six books. Over. Go out into the world and do something else. Be useful.'*

She had looked at me incredulously but stayed silent as she finished her tea. 'Thanks for the tea, Debika.' She picked up her bag and left.

I was in no mood to mollycoddle. Those were cruel words I had uttered. I was in the mood for cruel. Was I cruel because I felt helpless? That's no excuse. If I had apologised, she would have dismissed it and come around. But I didn't. I was so sure she would forget it and soon call me.

She never did.

Gul

Neelesh died early this morning. Poor chap. With Gul gone, I seem to grieve for others more. Like a black hole, my heart draws in all the darkness of this world into itself. Gul would have been shattered by this news. Neelesh was quite dear to her.

I still remember the day I first met him at the restaurant Gul had insisted on going. I still remember how she sulked when I said I wasn't up to driving across the city in the late-evening traffic. Dearest Gul. What will I not do to have you back with me now? What is a little drive? I could drive across the world just to be with you, to sit across a table from you and hear you talk between spoonfuls of your favourite mulligatawny soup.

We were ordering soup. She looked ethereal in a pea-green chiffon saree and some blue-green jewels sparkling subtly on her ears. She was peppy that night. But also a little disconcerted, perhaps. As we sat looking at the menu, someone stopped by at our table.

'Hello,' a short, dark man was looking at our faces by turns.

Remembering faces is not my forte, but Gul's face lit up in recognition. Turned out I hadn't met him before. She introduced us, mentioned some company he headed. Neelesh was leaving. He had come to dine with a business partner, who had just called in to say he would not be able to make it. So my beautiful Gul—sitting there before me in her pea-green saree and, what she told me, Pacific opals in her ears—the one who always knew what to do in any situation, asked him to join us. That's how I met Neelesh. Later, Gul did a lot of design work for his firm.

I miss Gul so much. No one comes by as much as they did when she was around. She was the life of this home. The laughter. The sunshine. She was the successful career woman who made sure there were hot phulkas on the dinner table, matching towels in the bathrooms, and never a decaying tendril on her lush-leaved plants. Even the raddi was stacked in neat piles and the kitchen napkins always four-folded—their edges tucked inside.

When Kailash, my childhood friend visited, he would leave the newspaper folded backward, inside out, as he liked to read the editorials last, aaram se. Gul, always the polite one, would ease herself seamlessly into the scene, asking some deep questions about the mind, joking about how he must charm his women students, or something else instantly engaging and, thus chatting, pick the paper up seemingly unmindfully, fold it neatly at the folds it came in, and press it down to make it look as though it had just been delivered, fresh and unread, and keep it back on the table.

By the third day Kailash, a psychologist, began to tease her in his mild manner, 'Why is it important for you to place the chair at this angle? Why do you insist on white sheets so much, Gul?' Then jokingly, he said one day, 'Gul, you know this can become an obsession. It can lead to anxiety and worse, depression. Just let things be today. Let's see if the world's still turning on its axis tomorrow morning, shall we?' She just smiled, fluffed up the cushions he had been reclining on and left for work.

One day he even said, 'You know, you must look inside more. What is bothering you? Set that right and all these external things will stop making you anxious.' She said, 'Yes, I will, Kailash. Thanks. But I must say you psychologist must stop reading too much into harmless behaviour.' Ms Neat Freak, he continued to call her.

But in her last days, it was tough on her. Her pain, her fast wasting away. She was only fifty. She just went to the hospital one day and never came back home.

Initially, the thought of her not going home, never occured to us. When I forgot to get the bottle of cologne that she had asked for, I said we could manage without it because she would anyway be home soon. Gradually, we began to say 'when you get back home', as if we needed to hear it out loud, to keep believing in it.

She said she was tired of the hospital lavender—lavender sheets, lavender screens, lavender gown. 'My eyes are pining for a dash of yellow.' That evening Neelesh got her a bunch of crisp yellow roses that the hospital did not allow inside. The only colour we saw next was the red of blood. A lot of it.

Sometimes, I feel she's still around.

That day when Neelesh came after her chautha, he just sat there in the aqua chair outside, his eyes still like the sea. He looked old and frail too. He always sat in that chair.

Gul and I had such a fight over that colour. When those cane chairs needed a fresh coat of paint, she got them painted aqua. I did not approve so when Neelesh came to drop her late that evening I mocked her. 'Where have you been with my lovely wife?' I had teased, shaking hands with him. Neelesh seemed embarrassed.

'Offo, think before you speak. It was nice of Neelesh to offer to drop me. No autos were ready to come this way,' Gul spoke instead.

She plonked herself ungracefully into the chair next to me and bunched up her feet under her like Neelesh wasn't around. Neelesh sat down too, and I asked Chotu to get water.

When Chotu came with the glasses, Gul said, 'Arre, you forgot? Get ice in one for Neelesh Saab.' She expected Chotu to remember the little things about our guests like she did. Dear Gul.

That night she asked him to stay for dinner. She went in for a shower while we talked over a few drinks. On other days, she'd come from work and sit on the veranda with me until dinner time. After dinner, she'd shower and immediately crash into bed.

But that day she came to the table bathed, her hair wet. She was wearing a pale pink Lucknawi kurta that made her skin radiant. She had laid the table beautifully with snowflake-shaped floating candles. My Christmas present to her.

How I miss all the beauty in her and our surroundings that she created. A single bunch of the humble magenta bougainvillea in the stout vase in the foyer; a spotless white damask tablecloth, a succulent in a bright ceramic pot on the coffee table, an old Moroccan lamp refurbished by fitting fairy lights inside, a warm rug here, a candle there, she could bring this house alive with her magic touch.

'How do you like the aqua chairs, Neelesh?' I was expecting a man's view, more akin to mine. More conventional, perhaps.

'Quite striking, I'd say.' He looked at them admiringly. I forgot he was a design guy. Not a 'regular' guy like me. I would have preferred a nice coat of varnish over the cane.

'I need change,' she had said. She always said—'I need change. I get bored.'

I must get to Neelesh's place now. Maybe I should wear the blue Fabindia kurta he got me last Diwali. We were not gift-exchanging friends, until one day at the handicrafts exhibition, Gul picked up a Tree of Life, kalamkari cloth painting. The muted vegetable colours of the tree were outlined with vibrant kantha work in pink, yellow, and blue. It was striking. Finally, she had found something for that foyer wall.

'I want to buy this for Neelesh. He would absolutely die of joy.'

Now they were both dead. Poor joke.

It is 11.30, but I'm not sleepy. I slept after returning from Neelesh's cremation. The children, Sohum and Shivam, touched my feet. Jyoti was dignified as always, the children by her side. Gul would have been able to comfort her. More the boys, I think.

I remember being a little surprised by how much she knew about the boys. Nonchalantly, while dropping ice into his glass she would say, 'But Neelesh, you must let Shivam buy that MacBook. He's been waiting for it too long.' Or, 'Has Sohum sent out his applications? Did you check that university, the link I sent you?' Gul was so much at ease around him.

Now that I think about it, Neelesh was eating with us almost daily. She'd be working late, he would come to drop her home, come in to say hello to me, I would ask him to stay for a drink and soon dinner would be on the table and the three of us around it.

After Gul left us, he rarely stayed for dinner. In fact, he never did. When he did come, once in two weeks, after two drinks, he would get up abruptly and say, 'I must be going now.'

I could say, dinner is ready, won't you join me. But I never did.

Was I more considerate of the wife waiting back home? Why is it that my thoughtful Gul never thought of her? Why did Neelesh never say, 'Jyoti must be waiting'? Why did he never say, 'I have to take Jyoti to a movie, dinner, stroll…'anything, anyplace?

But what is the point of all this now?

Finally, I sent out my scores for the short story competition this morning. And I'm coming to the end of T's book too. It has so consumed me that even though my attention was divided, I'm already wary of that familiar forlornness that suddenly weighs one down when a good book gets over, that void it leaves one with. T and I discussed this often. She called it a 'book hangover,' I thought of it as a 'withdrawal symptom.'

I cannot help but look for flaws in this collection, where only I, who understood the writer in her so well, could have helped elevate the nuances. There are none. Not a single aberration. She had a good editor. They may have become good friends too.

The award function for the short story competition is on Wednesday. T's launch is on the same evening I have to be at the award function for certain. Saves me much heartburn.

She'll soon be off to the US for her fellowship. I should call to congratulate her. Or I'll drop an email later. But that's about all I will do. If she wants to meet me, she will need to say that. Otherwise, well, life goes on.

Stuck Like Lint

He kissed her mouth again before lying down beside her, his head resting on her arm. She kissed his forehead. A butterfly kiss.

It was raining. She'd made him draw the sheer curtains. At such a height, they were safe from prying eyes but she was coy. From where they lay in bed, they couldn't hear the rain as it fell silently nine floors down, drawing a curtain of mist between them and the world.

'Time we dressed,' she said.

'Time is such a dog,' he said. She caught it and smiled—his not using 'bitch'. He knew her so well.

'You go first,' she said.

He got up and walked to the basin. Splashing water on his face, he picked up a fresh face towel and patted his face dry. He whistled his favourite song as he ran the comb through his hair. The flight back was in two hours. The overnighter stood packed on the luggage rack. They still had time for a coffee before they left.

They had coffee when she came in the morning. That's when she had said, 'We're in a mess'. He had stayed silent. What was there to say? It had started with a note *she* had written.

For me saying 'I love you' has become such a crucial part of this relationship. Does it mean a commitment? No. It's not as if I'm not going to want to say it to someone else in six months, or I won't go to see someone I've said it to, forgotten years ago. I just need to express what I'm feeling so overwhelmingly now, and over some time, and I need to let you know—so you can do something about it, if you want to—take it forward or keep quiet—glad in your heart, but knowing it would be the honourable thing to do, secretly hoping I would stay this way but assuming nonchalance, and telling me of the vainness of such.

I can't stop to think of what will work—for you, for me, or if God willing it is 'us' for a bit, on a certain road, which we're meant to walk together; then go, willingly, our own. There will be happiness and fulfilment and there will be heartburn, stuck to it like lint. Like all other cosmic connections of love—of mother, of friend—this too is meant to create new things in us, in our hearts and minds as we move onward, go through what we must in this life, evolve.

Commitment wasn't a condition then. Love is—now.

He looked at her lying in bed, the covers in soft white peaks around her. She was looking away at a distance through the curtains and the falling rain, perhaps at the hazy silhouette of the mosque dome painted in green stripes. She had once asked him if 'gumbad' was a tomb. 'Dome' he had told her and that the overlapping tooth, her left canine, was what he loved most. He walked into the bathroom.

She wasn't in bed when he came out. He imagined her sitting in the anteroom on the armless couch with her feet up—one folded and tucked under her as she hugs the other knee, her chin resting on it—a wistful look in her eyes that comes when it's time to say goodbye. Picking his shoes, he walked in to not find her there. The door to the balcony was slightly ajar and the drapes stood like transparent walls, still with wetness.

He watched her frame in a mist through the sheer curtains, the falling rain, her feet poised on the dripping railing like a ballerina's.

There is no response to my calls, messages or email. Maybe she's in transit, already on her way. Where do I begin? This is so emotionally shattering. I can't bear to think what it is like for T.

I was late for the awards function today and was quickly ushered in to the stage to speak. As I was speaking, I noticed a face in the audience that looked vaguely familiar. But then, there were many familiar faces in that audience. When the second prize was announced, this vaguely familiar face, whose name was Subhadra Kumar, came up to receive it. I still could not place her. She looked at me and smiled, as though she knew me. By then, my bird brain was hopping mad, trying to place her. She accepted her prize, got off the stage and disappeared.

After the awards were handed and speeches made, we went indoors for tea. I looked around for her because I had suddenly realised who she was. She was T's husband, Shekhar's cousin, Sue, who I had met at the play with T. Of course, she had disappeared. The story she wrote, the story that had won her the second prize, was the one that had played out in their lives.

The Trade Off

Leela ran barefoot in the lawn, the morning sun warm on her just-washed hair. Mukul would be back from school soon and then they would sneak into his uncle's room to look at the telescope. Mukul wants to take her there some night when his uncle is away. He tells her that the night sky is 'way beyond her imagination'.

The part of the lawn under the trees was slushy, so she turned back and ran to the apricot tree, jumped up to catch a smooth slender branch and began to swing from it, her green frock riding up her thighs.

In a couple of days, she would be back home and Mukul would also return to his parents. They were second cousins, enjoying their vacation with their grandparents. She came with her mother every year during summer and Mukul stayed with them during his school term as his father, who was in the railways was posted in a remote town. Everyone said they were two peas in a pod. Leela plucked a green, fuzzy apricot and bit into its bitter flesh.

'Yaaayyyeee!' Mukul came running through the gate, screaming. His school bag was hanging precariously at the end of his not-okay arm, and the loosened knot of his tie swung on his chest. The cook spotted him from the kitchen window and called out, 'Bhaiya, close the gate please, the goats will get in.' But Mukul was already on the porch taking off his shoes and flinging his bag and tie on the chairs. Still screaming, he ran into the lawn, slipped on the slush and fell flat on his stomach. 'Hahaha!' Leela laughed and ran to him. A clay Mukul!

'Give me your hand,' he said making little effort to rise. Leela stretched her hand out to him, remaining carefully on the dry grass. He lugged at her arm and in a trice she was in the slush too.

'Oh Mukul!' she whined, wiping the mud from her mouth with the back of her hand. She began to cough. Mukul ran to the far end of the garden and turning on the tap, dragged the coiled hosepipe to her. As the water spouted from it, he stood holding it so she could wash her face and rinse her mouth. Then a spray hit her hair without warning. She looked up. His eyes were twinkling with mischief. He clinched the mouth of the hosepipe so it squirted sharp jets of cool water on her. Leela shrieked with joy and began to run, not in the least wanting to escape the spray that followed her around the garden.

'Now your turn,' he handed the hosepipe to her. Such funny things Mukul did. Jumped and somersaulted and made weird faces. They were drenched and hungry. A scolding from inside the house seemed inevitable as they spotted some goats nipping off the rose buds near the gate.

During those long summer afternoons, when the elders shut themselves in, pulled thick curtains over closed windows and lay on white cotton sheets over reed mats, the two of them played in the scorching veranda, feeling no heat or discomfort.

So many things happened after that. Things that Leela didn't wish to recall. Over the years, with the next few inches she picked up, she lost contact with her best friend from those summer days.

He had made a brief appearance at her wedding, but she had been too caught up to spend any time with him. His presence was registered like that of many others. She remembered he had long hair, wore torn jeans, and talked with an accent on a fancy cell phone. He wasn't Mukul, her playmate, anymore. He was a very successful media director by then, whose phone never stopped ringing.

Leela and her husband had separated after five years of living acrimoniously and trying to adjust. She moved back to Gurgaon from NY, where Vikram had been on a posting. Gradually, as she came to terms with her single status, she got back to work and focussed single-mindedly on building a career. Mukul had connected with her on Facebook rather cursorily. He was married too. Mukul forgot to invite her to his wedding though. 'He forgot,' she thought wryly, but then realised that it was she who'd cut herself off from all relatives.

Now Mukul wrote to say that he'd be in Delhi for a meeting Friday and could she meet him for dinner. Leela offered to make dinner and invited him over to her place. He agreed.

Leela would be seeing him after 28 years. She was cheerful all day and hummed a tune as she set the table. She had taken care to look relaxed in a cotton tank-top and white linen pants, her hair held in a casual knot. When the doorbell rang, she stopped before the mirror to look at herself.

After so many years—and with no one else to fill the gaps of awkward silences—they were both ill at ease at first. Mukul spoke in spurts—'That's a nice painting'; 'Do you still sing?' Leela was quieter. So many childhood memories were suddenly alive and abuzz, but she waited. She needed to know if he wanted to venture there. Did he remember the same things? Did they still mean anything to him?

The beer helped. Mukul got up to look at the old family pictures she had put up on the foyer wall. 'Pinky masi! I met her last year at a wedding in Ambala. She has remarried. Oh, that's Bablu bhaiya, isn't it? Remember how we'd sneak into his room?' She remembered it all too well. Mukul stood without wincing even once while Bablu bhaiya beat him up mercilessly for entering his room in his absence and fiddling with his telescope. He would later brag to her that it was nothing, 'Bhaiya usually slaps the air, you know.'

'You know this lady next to your dad? That's my great aunt. What stories they would tell of her. It seems she had a secret lover. Every afternoon, she would sit on a chair under the jamun tree and talk to him on the other side of the boundary wall. Do you believe that? And that, the old maid bathing…is that *you*? She gave birth to babies every nine to ten months and none survived. The newborn would die within days, and she'd be back at work the next day…I myself counted ten. Do you know of my great grandmother's sister? She lived in Amreli. She gave birth to snakes. They were cared for as their children. There was also a deranged grand-uncle who was kept locked in a cage. Later, his mother was put in a cage next to his.'

Leela stood listening to him, nostalgia rising—memories of a wondrous childhood, the most beautiful time of her life.

Mukul slowly walked back into the living room and sprawled down on the carpet. He seemed more relaxed now. As he reached out for some ice on the table, Leela knelt forward to hand it to him and knocked over his beer mug. Horrified, she watched as the liquid form a large map on his tee. He looked up at her and she at once caught the glint in his eye—the familiar mischievous sparkle of a seven-year-old. He picked her mug one-fourth full and before she could react, emptied it down her head. The suddenness of it made her stand up and he broke into a booming laugh.

Taking her by the hand, he led her to the foyer and stood her before the mirror, 'Now you look like the Leela I remember.' She saw him standing behind her holding her by the shoulders and smiling. Her Mukul was back. She smiled at him in the mirror and then suddenly feeling awkward, said, 'I'll go change.''

Arre! It's okay! It'll dry up in five minutes.' He said. Beads of the fluid glinted like little jewels in her dark hair. 'Besides beer is good for the hair.' He tried to joke, but his eyes were deep as thoughts.

Standing so close to someone she had known from happy, carefree days, a sense of loss, her loneliness swept over her like a surging wave.

She closed her eyes to steady herself and felt his arms closing around her. He turned her around and held her close as she trembled with emotion, then holding her by the shoulders, kissed her forehead. 'Chipkali,' he said and suffixed it with a loud laugh. It was the name he called her by as he ran after her pulling her long plait. It made them smile and neutralised the charged atmosphere a little. She showed him the spare bathroom and went to her room to tidy up.

The evening had taken an unexpected turn. When both sat eating, the silence was not for want of words.

'Very nice,' Mukul said of the curry as she passed him some. But he grew quiet, even a little restless. When she got up to get the caramel custard, she knew he loved, he said, 'Don't bother, I'm not too much for desserts. Must leave now.'

Her heart plunged. 'Coffee?' She didn't want him to leave yet.

'Not really. I must leave. I have an early morning flight to catch.'

She walked him to the parking lot where his cab was waiting and stood some distance away as he woke the cabbie up. He walked back to her but kept a little distance between them, his hands in his pockets, 'Thanks Leela. It was wonderful catching up. Take care.'

'My pleasure. Come again.' Most formally, she replied.

He nodded and was gone.

She saw him on Facebook, a few days later, with Shubha, tagged in someone's wedding photos. She was stunningly angular, the fashionable halter neck blouse showed off her long neck and beautiful shoulders accentuated by her short cropped hair. Mukul had his arm around her. Leela felt the pang of loneliness that was beginning to surface after so many years.

Shubha in Del 2 launch her nw bk @ IHC, sat. C if u can make it—he texted her some weeks later.

Gr8! But sorry, i'm travelling ☹—she replied.

No worries. Nxt time then ☺—he responded.

She wasn't going anywhere. She scanned the Sunday newspapers for the event coverage. She looked up the IHC website. The launch had been mentioned almost everywhere. The Tuesday local supplement carried her photo.

Leela was meeting an old client from Bangalore for coffee. The client came with his CEO, a person she'd spoken with over phone several times. He had appeared curt but now came across as quite pleasant. When Mr Murty excused himself and walked away to take a call on his cell, Leela turned to James, her contact, 'You should have told me you were coming with him! She hissed.

'I didn't know till the last moment myself. When I said I was meeting you in the afternoon, he just declared he was coming along too. Anyway, you don't need to worry about him; he's quite impressed with you. And…let me tell you, he's going to make you an offer!'

'What!' Leela was incredulous.

Mr Murthy returned to the table just then and apologising again, sat down. Without preamble, he said, 'Leela, would you consider moving to Bangalore to head our Marketing?

As she tried to find appropriate words, he continued, 'You don't have to give me an answer right away. Here's an offer letter. I think you will be a valuable resource for our company. Think about it.' He handed her a sealed envelope.

James winked at her as she turned to him totally dumbstruck. They got up to leave and Mr Murthy shook her hand firmly, 'Bangalore weather is definitely better.'

It was after they left that she noticed Mukul's missed call on her cell that was on silent for the meeting. She called him back.

'Hiya girl, what up?'

'Hey, nothing. Just out of a meeting. Where you?'

'In Gurgaon, of course. Are you free for dinner tonight?'

'Yes!'

'Come home;' 'Let me take you out,' they spoke together and laughed.

'Come home. I insist.' Sitting in a restaurant and being all formal with Mukul did not appear appealing to her. 'And I have news!'

'Yeah? Tell, tell! You got engaged?'

'No! Let's meet first.'

'Seven?'

'Seven.'

More relaxed this time, they sat discussing work and relatives and sipping beer.

'I got an offer from a Bangalore firm.'

'Great! So?'

'It is very attractive. Would be a sensible career move.'

'Go for it, then. Congrats!'

'New city. Thinking.'

'Aha! Spoken like a girl! It's not Antarctica! And then, we're there. What's your worry?'

Leela became quiet. We. It jangled her.

'And why didn't you ever tell me you were writing stories too? You must meet Shubha. She would be able to help.'

Now it jangled full-on.

'I'm not looking at a career in writing. I'm quite happy with the work I do. Writing is something I enjoy immensely. So kind of...I'm not really looking out for help.'

'Right.' He seemed to have caught the indignation in her voice.

'Anyway, do give it a *seeerious* thought. Bangalore weather is to die for.'

He stayed back for desserts. She had nothing except some tender coconut ice cream in the fridge and he hated coconut. When she got the coffee, he was lying on the couch with his eyes closed. Sensing her presence he opened his eyes and looked at her, as if from a time long ago.

'Leela, you remember when you tried to hide inside Kamal Aunty's saree hanging out to dry and got all entangled and it tore, and we didn't tell anyone?'

'Yeah, the orange one. It was a beautiful saree too. Her favourite.'

'It felt so cool. We'd brush against her wet sarees drying on the clothes line. And remember when we saw the uncle, next door, in his puja room?'

Leela blushed. Uncle was praying with just his janeau slung across his torso. Many times during the later years she had wondered about him. Why was he praying without his clothes?

'Strange man. But I wonder why we felt so guilty having seen him like that.'

This time he insisted she not come downstairs to see him off. He gave her a slight hug at the door and repeated, 'Come to Bangalore.'

In September, Leela moved to Bangalore. Mukul was travelling that week. They invited her home on the Saturday he returned.

Leela had taken care to dress well, a little formally in a churidar-kurta, her long hair straightened to a gleam. Shubha opened the door in track pants and an almost-faded tee.

'Hi Leela! So good to see you.' She stood there staring at her, then hugged and kissed her warmly on both cheeks. Immediately,

Leela felt better. 'Kuku, look who's here!' Shubha called out as they stepped into their huge, beautifully done and warmly lit living room. 'Make yourself comfortable,' Shubha said to her and carried the flowers Leela had brought, inside.

Mukul peeped out from the kitchen and said, 'What you doing sitting there like a guest? Come right in and give me a hand.'

He had slivers of eggplant, pumpkin, onion, and zucchini heaped on a platter and was beating besan, holding the bowl awkwardly in his not-okay arm.

'Do this,' he handed her the bowl of besan and turned up the stove to heat the oil in the wok. Clearly, he was the one who wore the apron in the house. '

You shouldn't have bothered,' she said feeling sorry about him having to do the cooking.

'Bother? Nah, I love this. Usually, weekends are my cooking days. I mean, I do the cooking most of the time if we're eating at home but, during weekends, I make special meals. Today, I was craving for these vegetable pakoris. Hope it does not upset your diet or something.' He turned to look at her and Leela felt conscious of herself in her fitted kurta.

Shubha was on phone, talking loudly into it and laughing louder. 'No sweetheart, I didn't have to sleep with him for him to give me such a flattering review. Hahaha!'

A large container stood on one of the burners turned on low heat. It was sealed with dough around its mouth.

'Biryani?' Leela asked Mukul.

'Yes, I'm great at making biryani.'

'I love biryani.'

'Good. How's work?'

'Great. Thoroughly enjoying myself.'

'Let me know if you need help with anything. The house, set?'

'Yeah, almost. I like to do it aaram se.'

'Chal, now you take out some dhaniya chutney and ketchup from the fridge into those bowls.' He was deftly sliding in the last batch of pakoris into the hot oil.

They sat on the terrace.

'These are to die for,' Shubha stuffed another pakori into her mouth with a large gulp of beer, then dramatically raising her hand announced, 'Take a bow, pati.'

Mukul raised his mug to acknowledge.

'Hey Leela, you two had wonderful times together. Mukul's such a sucker for memories. I so envy you both when he tells me of your childhood. I had a terrible childhood. My brother-in-law who lived with us was such a creep.'

'Shubh, can you get some more ice for me, please?' Mukul interrupted her.

Shubha got up reluctantly. She came back with the ice tray and opening the box, thumped the back of the tray loudly so the ice fell noisily into it. She left the empty tray on the table where it began to form little wet marks and sat with her legs up on her chair.

'And that one, Kuku? That nude man praying? Just imagine! You two naughty little kids peeking into other people's houses. Hahaha!'

Shubha was like a rude intruder rummaging through the basket of their favourite playthings holding them up for laughs. Leela's joy in the evening was beginning to wane.

'It's nice outside. Would you like to eat here, Leela? Under the stars?' Mukul changed the subject sensing her silence.

'Yes, that would be nice,' Leela looked up at the white puffs of clouds drifting in the dark sky. There were no stars.

'Hey, tell me more about you two. Tell, tell! Did you have any big secrets? I know you played house and were a couple. Kissing cousins? Hehehe.' Shubha sat up straight in her chair, excited like a child.

'No Shubha, we did no such. We had a different childhood... a more innocent one.' He was curt.

They sat in a very oppressive silence for a while.

Shubha spoke again, 'Kuku, you never told me Leela was so beautiful.'

Mukul stared at her, not speaking. 'I mean, you two met very often in Delhi, no?' Shubha asked.

'Twice.'

Leela was feeling very uncomfortable now. She wished she had not come. But the evening ended without any further drama.

In the coming months, Shubha reached out to Leela, calling her often and dropping in at her office a couple of times when she was in the neighbourhood. She even took her to meet her close circle of friends. It made Leela very happy when Shubha asked to read the couple of stories she has published in magazines and said she liked them.

One weekend, Mukul called Leela and sensed she was sicker than she was admitting. Half an hour later, when she dragged herself out of bed to answer the doorbell, Leela found Mukul and Shubha at the door.

'Oh poor dear, you look so sick.' Leela heard Shubha's words and a helplessness that was just beginning to weaken her, brought instant tears to her eyes. The flu was making her feel horrible. Mukul looked serious, almost angry. As though it was her fault. Damn you, falling sick! She almost heard him swearing.

'Just pack some things and let's go home.' Mukul was looking about the house for things to do, to wrap up. As though it wasn't her home, Leela bristled.

His anger and irritation seemed to grow. She didn't want to go with them. 'I'll be okay. I'm so much better than yesterday.'

Mukul paid no attention to her words. 'You just tell Shubh what to pack. I'll go check the house. We leave at once.'

'It's alright really. I can manage.'

No one seemed to hear her. Shubha poked her head into Leela's bathroom and came out waving her toothbrush, as if to state that the resistance was futile.

Leela was deposited into their guest room and immediately Mukul got busy setting up the bedside table with drinking water and meds on a tray and a thermometer.

'I'll make tea. Shubh keep Leela's things in the cupboard,' he handed Leela's bag to her and walked out.

Shubha just took the bag from him and plonked it inside the cupboard, coming to sit next to Leela on the bed.

'How are you feeling?' Without waiting for her answer, she continued, 'There's a book release I have to go for now. Then there's dinner with friends. But Mukul's here. You don't worry one bit. I might be late, so I'll see you tomorrow morning, okay?'

'Thanks Shubha. This is very embarrassing. I feel like such a baby.'

'Uff, please conserve your energy now. We'll go over this later.' Shubha smiled and left.

Mukul came in with two cups of tea and some biscuits. Leela sat up. The ginger-pepper tea soothed her sore throat. Neither spoke. Shubha peeped in ten minutes later and seeing Leela sitting up, walked in swirling a big, bold patterned skirt, with a short cropped top and long bead malas.

'How?' she asked, her eyes twinkling.

Leela smiled, 'Lovely.'

'Thanks love, bye you two.' Shubha stepped out.

'See ya,' Mukul murmured.

A moment later, Shubha peeped in again, 'You two don't get naughty!' she waved her index finger at them.

'Darling, it will be a great help if you behave yourself tonight,' Mukul spoke with a straight face.

Leela was just beginning to regret coming there when she caught Shubha wink at her. It made her smile—a girlie camaraderie she had not experienced in years.

Mukul just kept sitting there, not talking. Tired of sitting up, the tea and the meds soothing her mind and body, Leela began to slump. She had opened her eyes slightly, when she felt someone's touch. Mukul was gently removing the extra pillows from under her head so she could lie down and sleep.

Of the next two days, Leela remembered little except for Mukul's angry face hovering over her; propping her up for milk or bread, or daliya or khichidi or meds; walking her back from the bathroom to the bed and sponging her burning forehead and feet with cool, cologne water when she was delirious with fever. Shubha was also there sometimes, doing all the talking, but Leela could recall none of it.

Wednesday morning, she woke up again having dreamt incessantly of being wed. She remembered how mummy had fretted over the superstition that dreaming of marriage symbolised imminent death.

Quickly, she showered and got into a pair of fresh tracks and tee. She tidied up her room, drawing away the curtains and opening the windows. By the time she made her bed and packed her stuff into her bag she started feeling weak and lay down again.

At six thirty there was a knock on the door, and Mukul entered with tea.

'Whoa! Someone's had a busy morning. Better?'

'Absolutely.' She took the tea things from him as he drew his chair next to her bed. 'Mukul, thanks so much for everything. Will you drop me home on the way to work?'

'You're not going anywhere today. You look too pale. I'm working from home.' He was firm.

'You don't have to do this, you know. I'm used to staying alone. I've been managing all these years.'

'That was then. Now you have me…us.'

Her throat constricted and eyes welled up. She'd never felt so vulnerable, so much in need of someone's love or care. What was happening to her? What had Mukul unleashed in her?

'Why are you doing this to yourself, Leela?'

'What?'

'You know what I'm getting at. You are too hard on yourself. Showing the world this tough girl exterior. Let yourself go, Chipkali.'

Warm, like the love-sadness that surged inside her, her tears flowed. Mukul pinched some tissue from the box and handed it to her, keeping one assuring, comforting hand on her arm but not looking. Shubha walked in yawning in her little night dress.

'What's up?' her eyes opened wide as she apprised the scene.

Mukul smiled 'Drama queen! She's crying 'cause she thinks we're going to ask her to leave now. Come, you sit with her, I'll get you tea.'

'Please yaar, stay here as long as you like. I'm sorry I'm not around much. What to do every day there something or the other. Tomorrow I'm going to Hyderabad for an event.' Even as she spoke with such apparent casualness, Shubha was looking at Leela intently. Leela felt the need to match her generosity with gratitude.

'I'm sorry for all the trouble, Shubha. You both have been so kind. I'm perfectly alright now. I will need to get back to work too. I must leave today.'

'In that case, Mukul can drop you while going for his meeting this evening.' Shubha was more direct.

Leela was exhausted when Mukul deposited her with her bag back home into her bedroom. She lay down immediately.

'I'm leaving,' he came to say after he'd kept some milk and bread in the fridge for her. She opened her eyes to say bye, but Mukul was a blur. She smiled, not wanting him to know. His angry look seemed to return.

'Are you okay? I can cancel the meeting, you know. It's nothing important.'

'I'm fine, just tired. I'll sleep now.'

'Okay. I'll come on the way back and if you're still not feeling okay, we'll go home.' And he disappeared.

He did not come. Leela slept a little, then took a long, warm bath and tidied up her place. She waited, feeling deserted. He had done an amazing lot for her, but when he said he'd come, he should have at least called to say he wasn't going to. She began to feel very angry, and when the doorbell rang at nine, she was ready to lash out at whoever was bothering her at that hour. Some residents' association notice needed her signature.

She returned to the kitchen, put two bread slices into the toaster and was rummaging through the cabinets for some ready-to-make soup when the doorbell rang again. Her nerves stiffened and she decided not to open the door. It buzzed again, longer. She stomped to the door, flung it open and was ready to charge.

'Sorry! The meeting just dragged on.' He didn't seem to notice her anger. 'How are you feeling?'

'Mad!' Leela was furious with the world. He was upsetting her. Why didn't he just stay away?

He slumped into the couch. 'Did you eat anything?'

'I am making soup.'

'I'll have some too.' He was totally blind to her anger. It made her want to shake him up.

He got a call on his cell and Leela went inside to check on the food. There were some frozen cheese fingers which she fried for him. She heard him talking on the phone and then he came to lay the table. 'Shubha called to say she'd be staying with friends tonight.'

As they sat eating, his assuring presence beside her, their elbows touching, she relaxed.

'You know Leela, Shubha and I—we get along so well as friends, but when it comes to being husband-wife, commitment, home, family, we have such contrary views. She's too much of a free bird and I'm such a homebody. In a way, I envy how you manage on your own like this. If I look back at that Chipkali, I would never have imagined then that you'd one day turn out like this.'

'Like what?'

'Fish, fish,' he smiled.

They cleared the table. He then asked if she was sleepy.

'No, actually I think I slept enough for a month in the last two days.'

'You bet. Like Kumbhkaran. Every time I came into the room, you were snoring.'

'Snoring? Never!'

'Really, I should have recorded. I should have known you'd never admit.'

He was standing very close to her behind the kitchen sink. Suddenly, she felt dizzy and gripped the ledge.

'Are you okay?' He was holding her…pushing the hair back

from her face...carrying her to bed. 'Oh Chipkali, look what you've done.' He stroked her back as she sat in bed feeling very ill.

The situation was overwhelming her. He was her cousin. He was married. He had to leave her and go. Helpless before the desire of her heart, she began to cry.

His voice rasped to a murmur. 'Leela?'

She sobbed into the pillow she was holding over her face, while he sat there stroking her hair, her back, talking to her, till she fell asleep.

'I love you, my Chipkali,' Mukul was murmuring into her hair.

At midnight when she woke up, Leela found Mukul sleeping next to her. It was so frightening that she sprang up from the bed. What had she done? What would she do now?

And yet, there was no one to turn to, except him. He had made the decision. She must too. What was the point of resisting now? Tired, she slumped back into bed and snuggling close to his warm body, falling asleep instantly.

Except when he was travelling, Mukul would come to her every day. Some evenings he left early, some nights he stayed back. Soon the guilt began to gnaw at her.

'We are cousins.'

'You care?'

'My conscience.'

'My love. Even if you didn't love me, my love alone would see us through.'

Sometimes, the sense of wrong would engulf her and then Leela would stop meeting him. She would tell him she was busy and would stay back late at work. He would insist on picking her up, waiting patiently in the car, parked in the lane outside her office. Some days, her happiness in his love, sequined her world, but suddenly, without warning, her soul would be gripped by guilt, when she saw herself as the victim. Wasn't this just very convenient for him? Wasn't he exploiting her? A lonely woman in need of love? She hated herself for being so weak and vulnerable.

'Will you marry me?' she would challenge him.

'I would love nothing more, my darling. But we cannot hurt others. Imagine what that will do to those close to us?' It became his stock reply.

Sometimes, when she stopped taking his calls and told him she wanted out, he let her be. After a few days he would call, as if nothing had happened, and by then she'd be too desperate to be back with him. He would only say, 'I was waiting, darling.'

When Mr Murthy began operations in Delhi, he asked if she wanted to move back there and she refused. Mukul said she did right.

Whenever Shubha was around, he played the perfect husband. Sometimes, after being with them at their place, Leela would return feeling bitter and wanting to end her relationship with Mukul once and for all, but then her phone would ring and Mukul would tell her how much he missed her.

One Saturday afternoon, when Mukul was out of town, Shubha came to Leela's place unannounced.

As they sat down with tea, she asked, 'What's your plan, Leela?'

'Plan?'

'Are you in Bangalore for good?' Her words were cold.

'I haven't thought about it. I definitely like it here. The job's great.' She smiled with effort.

'Of course.' Shubha only said that. It did feel as though she had implied more. An awkward silence followed.

'Are you writing something, Leela?'

'In fact, I just finished a collection of short stories. I was wondering...' Even as she blurted it out, relieved that Shubha had switched to a more affable matter, Leela worried that she had spoken too soon.

'Great! Why don't you give it to me to read? I'd love to. And then I can also put you in touch with my publisher.' Shubha suddenly brightened up.

'I think, I will sleep over it for a bit.'

'Come on! Let me read. I'll tell you.'

Leela felt cornered. For the past six months, she had worked laboriously every night, writing her stories. She wanted Mukul to be the first one to read them. That morning, she had printed the whole manuscript, filed it neatly and kept it on her desk, waiting for Mukul to return on Wednesday and read it.

She had imagined him sitting there on the couch with his reading glasses perched at the tip of his nose, his left foot over his right knee, reading her stories while she buzzed about him, cooking his favourite meal, getting food on a spoon for him to taste and kissing him sloppily, suddenly. A picture of perfect domesticity was all she dreamed of these days.

'You have it on your laptop?' Shubha broke in.

Without another thought, Leela went in, got the file and handed it to Shubha.

'Wow! Neat! Great yaar, Leela. I will read these and tell you soon. Chal, I must leave now.

Wednesday evening, Mukul came carrying a big box; a little child's excitement lit in his eyes. He went straight into her balcony asking her not to come until he called. About half an hour later, during which she restlessly flitted about the house, she heard him from the balcony, 'Come, Chipkali.'

He stood next to a telescope he had installed for her and held her close. They looked at the night sky, oblivious to the world around them, their unusual circumstances.

Shubha called.

Mukul spoke choosing his words carefully, all the while running his finger into Leela's hair. His wedding band glinted in the muted light. He said he was just leaving a client's place and would eat at home. Leela stiffened. She had made lasagne for him.

Tonight, she had planned to tell him about the stories. The stories that were in his home now. But she didn't want to share any excitement with him anymore. The resentment was back.

He did not make any attempt to placate her, just kissed the back of her neck as she stood turned away, 'Love you, darling,' he said and left.

Two weeks went by and Mukul did not mention the stories. Leela did not ask. She was eagerly waiting for Shubha's call.

'What's Shubha busy with these days?' she asked as he lay on the sofa, his head in her lap, his eyes closed in relaxed contentment.

'Oh, this and that. But now that you ask, I remember her asking me several times recently if I've met or spoken with you.'

'And have you?' Leela teased.

'No, unfortunately, I have been too caught up with work.' He pulled her face close and kissed her.

Unable to wait longer, early in office one morning, Leela called Shubha, 'How are you? Have you been busy? Could you find time to read my stories?'

Shubha sounded preoccupied, 'Yes, I did. In fact, I was planning to call you. Let's meet for coffee outside your office at four?'

'You didn't like my stories?'

'Let's meet. I'll tell you.'

'Four then. See ya.'

'Arre, before I forget, send me the soft copy.'

'Okie!'

'Will you send it to me now?'

'Right away.'

Leela spotted Shubha sitting at one of the tables outside, under a tree. She was smoking and appeared deep in thought.

'You look chic. Navy suits you.'

Shubha looked up and took in Leela's formal dress suit. Leela wanted to return the compliment but couldn't find anything to say except, 'Thank you. You look tired, what's up?'

Shubha did not speak. She kept smoking. They ordered coffee. Shubha looked straight into Leela's eyes and in a very steady, unfluctuating voice, said, 'The night you went home from ours. The night I was apparently staying with friends, I did not go. I was home. Waiting for Mukul to return.'

She said no more just kept puffing at her cigarette and determinedly looking away.

Leela sat frozen. Her heart beating so hard, it drummed in her ears. Husband snatcher. The Other woman. Whore. Their hopeless game was up. Her lie lay exposed. She would have to go away. Leave the two of them and make a dishonourable exit. How naive she'd been! And Mukul? Shouldn't he be sitting here now, answering this? Confronted by his wife, Leela knew that for the sake of both, herself and him, and for Shubha too, she must try refuting the allegation. She, slut, needed to lie.

'There is nothing…'

'I understand your need to deny it.' Shubha kept looking away. And at once Leela knew she would not be able to pull this off.

'Shubha…I'm sorry.'

'You are nothing to me, Leela,' Shubha turned to her, her glance cold and fixed. 'You are an outsider. But he is my husband.

He cheated on me. What he has done cannot be reversed and I can never forgive him.'

There was a momentary glint of tears in Shubha's eyes. But she held them back resolutely. Her gaze turned hard as she stubbed her cigarette, bent down and took out the file with Leela's stories from her bag.

'You took away everything from me, Leela. Kuku was everything to me. Go, you both! Do whatever you want with your lives. I'm going away. And I am taking these.' She clenched the file tightly in both her hands, got up and left.

Acknowledgements

Dinesh, from who I learned that all escape is within; Anando, sometimes the voice of the angel but mostly that of the devil on my shoulder; Shibani, the gentle nudger, the private idiom partner. They help me fly, every time. They are, all three, tireless readers of manuscripts. The mention here will prompt their rare drama skills—eye rolls.

I am grateful for the indulgent circle of friends and family who I don't always tell how much they mean to me; and for my Arushi family for their patience every time I take time off for my writing.

I owe immense gratitude to my friend, Jayanth Kodkani for his unfailing encouragement; my agent, Preeti Gill for her guidance and friendship; and my editor, Jayalakshmi Sengupta for her discerning editor's eye and shared joy in this book. Heartfelt thanks are due to the book-passionate team at Niyogi Books, who have reaffirmed my belief in 'nice'.

Courtesy: Shwetaa Sinha

Shefali Tripathi Mehta is a Bangalore-based independent writer and editorial consultant for e-learning courseware. Author of *What Were They Thinking!*–a book on observational humour–and co-author of *Ek Prarthana,* a coffee-table book, she has published short stories and poems online and in anthologies. Shefali writes on social issues, travel, parenting and disability awareness in newspapers and journals. She volunteers with the charity, *Arushi* and curates Gond art to support tribal artists.